MW00614455

Platonic Rulebook

SAXON JAMES

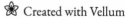 Created with Vellum

About this Book

GRIFF:

Walking away from my marriage was my idea of a fresh start.

My kid is in college, my ex-wife and I are on good terms ...
but being single in my forties is a world different to being
single in my teens.

I'm thankful for my best friend, Heath. He's got my back
like he always does and is ready to take me out and show me
how the bachelor life is done.

He was never supposed to show me *literally*.

After we wake up in bed together, I can't stop looking at
him differently, and one thing becomes abundantly clear.

I talk a big talk about wanting to be single, but my platonic rule book has gone out the window.

HEATH:

When my best friend comes to me for help post-divorce, I'm only too happy to impart my wisdom to him.

After all, Griffin isn't my type, but even I can tell he's a complete lumber*snack*. Good with his hands, kind eyes, and a killer smile. All the guys and gals are gonna eat him alive.

But the more time we spend together, the less "not my type" he becomes. *I'm* the one who can't get enough of him.

Neither of us is interested in a relationship, so what's a little fun between friends?

We both know the score.

Prologue

GRIFF

Even though I've had eighteen years to prepare for this day, I'm still not ready.

Ready to get out of this car, sure. Spending a week driving from Massachusetts to California sounded great in theory, but all it's doing is prolonging the inevitable.

Poppy and I wanted to give Felix one last family memory, a united send-off to college, because on his first break home, we'll be dropping the news of our divorce on him, and I have no idea how he's going to take it.

I love my son to pieces, but he tends to make a bigger deal out of things than is necessary.

By the time we reach Franklin University, there's a knot the size of the country sitting in my gut and one large enough to rival it lodged in my throat.

Felix will be staying in the dorms for his freshman year, and hauling his things up to his room is adding that extra stamp of finality to the occasion.

For the last eighteen years, he and Poppy have been around every day. I've loved them and looked out for them. Woken up every morning to my family and gone to sleep knowing they're safe.

But as soon as we leave here, I'll be catching a flight back to Kilborough while Poppy makes the drive. Even though we're both on the same page about the split, she didn't want to be around to see me move out, and I'm grateful for that.

She leaves us to head back out to the car, and I pause in the doorway of Felix's room. He's hunched over a box, clearly checking for something, and he glances up to find me watching him.

"Dad ..." he says in warning.

I hold up a hand. "I'm fine."

"You're not. You're going to cry. And then I'll cry. We made a *deal*."

We did make a deal. Which is why I force a smile even though that lump is getting bigger. I'm not a crier. It's not that I think men shouldn't cry or anything like that—there just isn't a lot that moves me to spontaneously leak from the eyeballs—but today ... it's a bit much.

Felix is grown up, and my marriage is ending all in one day.

None of it should be catching me by surprise, and yet ... here we are.

"Nope, no tears here," I say.

He gasps and points at me. "Your eyes are watery."

"Nope."

"And your voice did that wobbly thing."

I snort. "Now you're hearing things, kid."

The smile slips from his face, and his bottom lip shakes. "Dad ..."

I hold up a hand. "Dammit, Fe."

"Dammit, *me*? Dammit, *you*, old man." And unlike me, Felix *is* a crier. He pushes to his feet and crosses the room to yank me into a hug.

I immediately close my arms around him, and wetness hits my shoulder. "For the record, neither of us is crying."

He sniffs. "It's allergies."

"Of course." He doesn't have allergies.

"Hay fever."

"Obviously."

"You and Mom will be happy without me there to cramp your style."

My chest seizes, and I consider, not for the first time, how he's going to feel about us keeping this from him. The divorce has been on the cards for a long time now. We've been to counseling to try to save our marriage, but all counseling showed us was that the type of love we feel for each other isn't enough to sustain a relationship. We've spent the last year hiding our separation from Felix, not wanting to tell him until we can split for real and make sure this is what we actually want.

"Can I get in on that?"

I glance over Felix's head to see Poppy watching us. We break our hug long enough to pull her into the circle.

"My little boy is all grown up," she says. Unlike us, her voice is steady. Unfailingly practical and optimistic to a fault. "But that still doesn't give you permission to get anyone pregnant."

"Okay, okay." Felix pulls back and quickly turns away from us. "I think that's everything."

"Yep." Poppy points to the box she just brought up. "That was the last one."

"Right." I shove my hands in my pockets. Behind us, people are passing in the hall, and I look toward the other side of the room, where the bed stands empty. Felix has been chatting with his roommate for the last few weeks, but he obviously hasn't shown up yet.

"You'll be okay?" I ask him.

"Please." He waves a hand. "Give me a few days and I'll have so many friends I'll forget to call home altogether."

"Don't you dare," Poppy and I say in unison. We share a quick smile.

"And when you call, I'll be all *Dad who*?" Felix always uses sarcasm to make himself feel better.

I step closer to press a kiss to the top of his curls. "Enjoy yourself, and let us know if you need anything."

Poppy hugs him again. "You're across the opposite side of the country to us. I can't protect you as easily when you're so far away."

"I'll be fine."

"He will be," I say, forcing my voice to stay level. And I believe it. Felix might be small and dramatic, but he can hold his own, and I've never known him to need protecting.

We leave reluctantly, and Poppy drives me to the airport and has lunch with me before my flight. We're both subdued, thinking of everything we've had together and what's coming next.

When we finish eating, she lets out a long breath. "It's going to be strange to get home and have it half empty."

"I know. I'm still trying to wrap my head around it." I hesitate a minute. "We're definitely making the right choice, aren't we?"

"Yes. We've been through a lot, and it ... well, we have a few months to trial it, but I think we both know it's over."

I turn my wedding band round and round on my finger. "I didn't expect it to be this hard."

She laughs. "Don't go getting emotional on me now. I might want to keep you."

I chuckle, not feeling it, and she reaches over the table to take my hand.

"You're a man of habit, Griff, but it'll be okay. You were an amazing husband, but we were young when we got together. Now we'll be here to support each other for whatever is next. Plus, you know Heath will have your back for anything."

"I know." I squeeze her hand back. "It'll take some getting used to."

"It will. Starting now." With a sad smile, her fingers close over my ring, and she slowly pulls it off.

"Suppose it had to be done sometime."

"And I'll be very surprised if Heath isn't already waiting for you to land so he can take you on your first bachelor night out."

I run an unsettled hand back through my hair. Am I desperate to get laid again? Fuck yes. It's been too long since I had sex with anything but my hand. The problem is, I've only ever been with Poppy. I've been telling my friends for months now about how I can't wait to live up the single life, a different man or woman in my bed every night, and now that time is here ... I have no clue what the hell I'm doing.

How do people find each other these days? Do we date? Meet at a bar? Am I too old for clubs or apps?

"One other thing," Poppy says.

I tilt my head.

"I want you to have Magnolia Ridge."

"Wait ... what?"

We bought an old motel fifteen years ago and converted it into luxury accommodation. As much as I'd like to say we run it together, in reality, she and my best friend, Heath, run the place while I do the grunt work. General repairs, maintenance, gardens. I have nothing more than a basic idea of how to manage the books. This is ... not good.

"Why?" I ask once I'm able to process what this means.

"It was your idea and your dream. And yes, I'm good at it, but I want to take some time to work out what I want."

I can't say that's not fair, but fucking hell.

"You don't need to look so panicked. Of course I'll show you everything you need to know, and Heath isn't going anywhere. You two are joined at the hip anyway—you might as well run the place together. Besides, I'll still be around, but as more of a ... silent-partner-type situation."

"So you still want the money but none of the responsibility?" I can't help the question.

Poppy's face pulls tight. "Think of it as the vacation I never took. We'll work out logistics once things settle, but I do want to start pulling away. In whatever capacity that is, we'll work it out."

My head is still goddamn spinning, but I say the only thing I can. "Okay."

It's time for me to leave, and we reluctantly stand.

Poppy pulls me into a hug. "I love you, Griff."

"You too."

We part, and she gives me a cheeky look. "I'm sure this time tomorrow it'll be all *Poppy who*?"

"I'm not Felix."

"No, but you two are very similar."

I think of the five-foot-nine spitfire we dropped off. "Similar?"

"Neither of you likes change, even when it's for the best."

"Good thing we have you to give us that little push."

"Had," she corrects. "You're going to have to push yourself now."

"Fair call."

"Bye, Griff. Don't be home when I get back."

I laugh, because even though she's joking around, we both know there's every chance I might be. She's right about me being stuck in my ways, but now it's time to change that. I just need the guts to try.

Chapter One

HEATH

"You've been at Magnolia Ridge a long time," Marcos says, piece of paper loosely hanging from his fingertips. "Why the change now?"

Why now? "I hate job interviews" probably isn't the response he's looking for.

Being forty-three and having one job for twenty years with no hopes of career progression just sounds sad.

Mentioning that his job is closer to Mom and before Dad died I promised I'd keep an eye on her sounds morbid.

But saying that the only reason I've stuck it out at Magnolia Ridge for so long is because I didn't want to leave my best friend is plain pathetic.

Hmm ... which stellar answer do I go with?

"It's the right time for something new."

Marcos jots something on his paper. "Well, I can't deny

you have extensive experience. And, if I may, you are doing far more than the role of guest relations liaison usually expects."

I give him what I hope is a winning smile. "I like to take initiative." Am I ridiculously overqualified for what I'm paid? There's no doubt about it. But until Dad passed a few months ago, there was nowhere else in the world I wanted to be. I do extra because I *want* to. I'd get bored otherwise.

Marcos stands, and I hurry to mirror him.

"Thank you so much for coming in," he says, shaking my hand. "I was eager to meet with you, and I have a good feeling."

"Thank you. Hopefully I'll hear from you soon."

Marcos smiles. "We have a few things we're working on —background stuff, nothing to worry about—so it may be a few weeks before I'm able to get back to you, but you'll hear from me either way."

"That sounds great."

I leave the Premier Hotel, and while overall I know I smashed that job interview, I don't feel great about it. Moving to Southbridge closer to Mom cuts my drive time by a lot, or I could move in with her and make sure she's looked after as she gets older ... but it means leaving my own life behind.

I have friends and history in Kilborough. I love it there. It's not far from Springfield when I want to go out and get drunk or laid, or go to the gym, but it's far enough away from everything that the small-town life is perfect. Even during tourist season, it doesn't lose the feeling of home.

I'm sure Southbridge is great.

But it doesn't have my apartment and life. It doesn't have Griff.

Leaving him will be the hardest. We've been best friends from the moment we met, and even though we see each other every day at work, we also make plenty of time for each other on the weekends as well.

At least we did until I started using weekends to visit Mom.

I kind of miss him, even though I still see him all the time.

But over the past year, Griff hasn't been himself. He's been waiting. Almost like he's in this gray void waiting to start living again.

And today is that day—I hope.

Griff flies in tonight from dropping Felix at college, and the official breakup between him and Poppy starts. Even though they haven't been together for … a year? Officially, anyway. He hasn't had an opportunity to enjoy the split.

I'm going to get my boy drunk and laid.

I'm going to remind him that divorce is nothing more than the next step for him.

And I'm sure as hell going to be here to get him through it all … at least until I hear back about this job.

I groan, feeling that familiar split opening up inside me again. Griff needs me to get through this divorce. Mom needs me so she isn't alone, and as she gets older, it's getting harder for her to do the things she used to be able to. I promised Dad. It was one of the last things we talked about.

And yet, I'm still so fucking torn.

Selfish ...

I try to ignore the voice. I'm not selfish ... mostly. But this indecision is starting to change my mind about who I am deep down if I can't give up a little comfort to move an hour or so away.

I'm trying.

I applied for the job, I interviewed, I'm taking the steps I need to in order to keep my promise and look after my mom. My parents have always been amazing, I had the best childhood, and the least I can do to thank them for that is to make sure Mom doesn't feel alone.

I climb into my car. There's just enough time for me to get to the airport before Griff's flight lands.

There's no point stressing about the future. If Marcos says no, that's problem solved. If he says yes, I'll take it as a sign from the universe that Southbridge is my next step.

He's going to say yes.

That thought isn't at all reassuring.

DMC Group Chat

Griff: *It's done. Just like that. Twenty years gone.*

Art: *Incorrect. Those twenty years were simply Act I. Time for Griff 2.0 to emerge.*

Payne: *Kinda makes him sound like a cyborg.*

Griff: *Hey, if I had a robotic arm it'd probably be a talking point at least.*

Orson: *Ignoring that odd segue, how do you feel?*

Griff: *... confused? Like I'm sadder than I expected but maybe that's just what I think I should feel? Objectively there's nothing to actually be sad about.*

Orson: *It's a big change. Emotional turmoil is understandable.*

Payne: *Still think you made the right choice?*

Griff: *Definitely. Which is why the sadness is odd. Time to get laid, I guess! What's Beau up to later ;P*

Payne: *No more jokes about Beau.*

Orson: *You don't need to minimize your feelings. Take your time.*

Art: *Don't listen to them! You were right! Time to get laid!*

Chapter Two

GRIFF

There are two types of fliers. Those who barely notice we're twenty thousand feet away from solid ground and those who are way too aware of the fact.

I'm the first. The man beside me on the flight back was strongly in the second camp. I don't think I'll ever get the smell of vomit out of my nostrils.

By the time I leave the departure gate and look around for Heath, all I want to do is head home for a long shower before bingeing all the TV I can stand. I'm someone who's not good with being stationary, but I *am* good at sticking my head in the sand, and the longer I put off thinking about the shit that comes next, the better.

If I start thinking about the future too hard, dread

creeps in at the realization that I have no idea what I'm doing. I've had so many self-imposed rules in my life that were directly tied to my family, and now I'm running solo, the thought of all that freedom makes my head spin.

I rub my forehead, the start of a headache kicking in, and try to shake off the uneasiness.

A familiar loud whistle pierces the air. "Yo, Griff."

I turn to the voice, spotting Heath standing halfway across the room with his hand in the air. Not that it's needed. Heath is taller than most people, lean, and with hair so light brown it blends in with his skin.

You take one look at him and think *polished*.

You take one look at me and think *undomesticated caveman*.

He's wearing a button-up and holding his phone in one hand, the other lightly tucked into the pocket of his slacks.

"Been at work?" I ask.

"Yep. I got in a half day before leaving Michelle with the afternoon shift so I could visit Mom and pick your lazy ass up."

"And my lazy ass thanks you. How is your mom?" It's still hard to believe his dad is gone. I wasn't super close with his parents, but they were always around during our high school years.

"She's good-ish. Acts like herself most of the time, but she misses him, you know?"

"I couldn't even imagine." Losing Poppy would be hard even with the split, and losing Heath ... it'd feel like a part of me suddenly stopped existing.

"Enough of that." Heath slings his arm around my shoulders, steering me in the direction of the exit, and I'm hit with his sweet-smelling cologne. "I hope you got lots of sleep while you were away."

"You know I didn't." I've been texting him the entire last week. "Why?"

"I have something planned for tonight."

I force a smile. Poppy was right, and whether it was a lucky guess on her behalf because she knows Heath or if he told her, I can't be sure, but it doesn't matter. I should have known this was coming.

"Not tonight. Tomorrow, maybe," I say.

"Oh, big guy, I'm not giving you a choice here."

"What do you want for me to get out of this? Extra days off? To take over Magnolia Ridge? Just say it and it's yours."

"Take over your baby?" He sounds confused.

I wave the question away. "We'll talk about it later. For now, I'm going home to switch off."

"That's a great plan."

"I know."

"Too bad I can't let you do that."

I shrug off his arm. "It's been a day."

"I'm sure it has been, but too fucking bad." Before I can reply, he holds up his hands. "Don't shoot the messenger."

"Messenger? I thought you planned this?"

"*Details.* My point is, all of your friends are waiting at the Killer Brew, and they're going to be pissed if you don't make it to your own bachelor debut."

My head drops back. "You didn't."

"Oh, but I did. Obviously."

I try to shoot him another unimpressed stare, but it only makes him grin. I can't help but smile back.

"Griff, we've been friends since high school. No point pretending to be surprised now."

Well, that's true. When it comes to work, Heath's the ultimate professional. It's why he helps Poppy with so much of the business side of things, but outside of work, he's a player who never takes life seriously.

Heath leads me through the parking lot to his car, and twenty minutes later, we're on the road, leaving Hartford behind and heading home to Kilborough. I relax into the seat of his BMW M2, wondering whether it's time for me to dye my hair and buy a sports car as well. Is this divorce the start of my midlife crisis? Will Felix assume that's what's going on?

I catch a glimpse of myself in the side mirror of the car, and I don't like what I see. Sure, I don't look like an old man, but the grays are starting to creep in, the lines around my eyes and mouth are becoming more pronounced, and I look ... tired. That's not even taking in the extra weight I'm carrying.

"I can hear you thinking from here," Heath says.

Of course he can. I turn to see what forty-three looks like on him compared to me. The only grays he has sit at his temples. He's fit. Handsome. *He* doesn't look tired.

It's obvious why he never has an issue picking up.

"Tell me I can at least head home and change first?" It's

already past seven, and I'm scared he's going to push for me to go out in clothes that smell like plane puke.

"I'm so generous, I'll even let you shower."

"Which I'm sure is all for me and has nothing to do with you not wanting to smell me all night."

He wrinkles his nose. "I wasn't going to say anything, but dude, what is that?"

"Over six hours on a long-ass flight is what that is."

"Well, yeah, you definitely need to shower. No one is going to want to be around you smelling like that."

There's something in the way he says "no one" that gets my suspicion up. "Who did you invite to this thing?"

"Eh, you know ... the usuals."

I hum. "Like ..."

"Some guys from school, your divorced friends ..." He drops his voice to a low murmur. "A couple of hot dudes from the gym in Springfield."

And there it is.

"*What*?" he asks. If I could make out his expression behind his large sunglasses, I'm sure he'd look offended. "You've been saying you want to hook up."

I don't answer because I don't know what to tell him. I have been saying that, to pretty much anyone who will listen, and it's not all talk either. I'm long overdue for being with someone, and I'm craving it. Poppy and I never consciously made the decision to stop having sex, but we did agree not to see other people while we were still living together. It was mostly to make sure Felix didn't catch on to any rumors and also to spare each other from having to see our ex with someone else.

We swing by my soon-to-be old home, and I take my time getting ready. Even though I'll know the majority of people there, nerves are threatening to take over. I'm all for throwing these parties since Art loves them so much, but when they're thrown for *me*, I'd rather tap out.

We get to the Killer Brew around eight thirty, and even for a weeknight, it's busy. I shuffle my feet as Heath leads the way into the large wood-and-steel brewery, trying to work out exactly how sick I'll need to fake in order to get out of this. Before I can try anything though, Heath's hand closes over the back of my neck, and he steers me toward the stairs behind the bar.

Just his presence is a constant source of comfort. It helps me fake confidence.

"You can quit shitting yourself now."

"Until you've been to a party celebrating your divorce, you don't get to give advice."

He lets go of my neck and cuffs my shoulder. "I'm not dumb enough to get married, so nothing to worry about there."

"I dare you to tell Poppy she was a dumb choice."

"What ... no, that's—"

I laugh at his spluttering. "Careful, you almost sound scared of her."

"That's because she *is* scary."

"Uh-huh." Poppy is tiny. She's where Felix got his height and build from.

"Don't act like you're not scared too," he says. "We knew who wore the pants in that relationship."

I pause halfway up the stairs to the mezzanine level, where Art holds our catch-ups and parties. Since he owns the place, he has free rein over whatever happens here. I can already hear the loud conversations of the people above, and once again, the feeling of being totally overwhelmed creeps up on me again.

"Griffin." Heath squeezes my shoulder. "You're okay. I'm here."

I breathe out the anxiety. "Yeah, I know."

"The sooner you get back out there, the easier it will be."

I send a quick smile his way. "It almost sounds like you knew I'd be nervous about this."

"Nervous? You? Never." He slaps me on the back. "Come on, you big ol' lumbersnack. I'm just glad you left your flannel shirt behind."

I flip him off because I don't *always* wear flannel shirts, fuck you very much. They're a practical option when I spend the day getting my hands dirty.

As soon as we walk into my *bachelor debut*, a cheer rumbles through the room. I lift a hand, trying not to cringe under the attention.

"The day has come," my good friend, Art de Almeida, says as he approaches. He pulls me into a rough hug, then leaves one arm around my shoulders and waves the other toward the people gathered. "You know how to keep a room waiting."

My cheeks grow hot. "I didn't know there was a start time."

"I mean the last year, you son of a bitch. How does it feel? You're finally joining the A-league. Free to spread your wings and soar into the next stages of living."

Sometimes, I wish I'd see life the way Art does. Other times, I wish he'd lower his voice and not draw attention with all his hippy-dippy views on life.

"It feels ... odd."

"Sounds about right. This still what you want?"

"Yes." I clear my throat. "That part I'm sure of." Even if I have moments of not being sure, it's not because I want to stay married. The divorce is the smart choice.

"So," Art nudges me, "any of these dudes catching your eye? Are you finally gonna get some dick?"

"I'm not fussy, you know that." I've been low-key out as bisexual since I figured it out about myself in my early twenties, but I've only ever been with Poppy. For me, men and women fall equally in attractiveness. The goal moving forward isn't to tick off a list of body parts to touch. I only want to have sex. Casual sex. As long as they're cool and I'm attracted to them, that's all that matters to me.

I think.

With this hitting me too much too soon, I still haven't worked out where my head is at. Picturing a random dick is intimidating, but so is picturing a random pussy. When you've only ever been with one person all your life, it's hard to imagine doing those things with someone else. I'm genuinely lucky to have the massive support system that I do. This is a rough patch, but I know I'll get through it. Maybe I'm not built for hookups, or maybe I'm not used to them yet because I've never done them.

But I'm going to try.

Because the very last thing I want is to fall into another relationship.

Chapter Three

HEATH

Griff is freaking out. Right on schedule.

I throw back what's left of my beer and watch him interacting with his friends. He's been getting more and more vocal about the divorce in the last few weeks, and I knew it was only to cover his nerves, because right now, he's barely holding it together.

I check my watch for the thousandth time, still torn about coming out tonight. I always knew this would be a struggle for Griff, but I also know it's because he gets so in his head about things. If I'd let him off easy, it'd take weeks for him to gain the courage to leave the house.

As soon as I get the cute bartender's attention, I order two more beers. He's been here for a few months now, and he's nice to look at. Lean muscle, hair pulled back into a short bun, and a wicked smile. He also flirts up a storm, but

I know from experience that flirting goes nowhere unless you have a set of boobs.

"There you go, cutie," he says, sliding the drinks toward me. And it's a damn shame he doesn't swing my way because that voice always catches my interest.

I hand over my money, lips quirking at his confidence. "Keep the change."

I cross the room toward Griff. My plan tonight is to be here when he needs me but not let him use me as a crutch. Give him space, then remind him I'm here and repeat. He's a grown-ass guy, but he's adorably naive.

I'd protect that man with my life.

The problem is, Poppy did everything for him. She's a firecracker. Someone who's not happy being still, and nothing is ever too big for her to handle. She runs the business with military precision and still manages to do all the domestic stuff that goes with having a family as well. Some days I felt sorry for her because of Griff's lack of help when it came to cooking or cleaning, but she told me one day that she couldn't give up the control.

And I thought he'd been exaggerating when he said he couldn't do anything right.

Well, he's going to be paying for that now.

I bump his elbow when I reach him and hold out his beer. Those vivid blue eyes catch mine, and sweet relief crosses his face. My lips twitch. I've been there for him since high school, and by this point, we can basically communicate without words.

Thank fuck you're back, his look tells me. *Help.*

I cock an eyebrow. *Stop sulking, you gigantic man child.*

He gives me an almost smile before rolling his eyes and turning away.

"I'm surprised you're here, actually," Payne Walker says. "I thought you would have headed straight to a club from the airport. Get that first hookup out of the way." He's the newest member of their divorced club and only moved back to town a few months ago. The guy is sex on legs, and if he and Beau hadn't gotten together so quickly, I definitely would have tried to sleep with him.

"All in good time," Griff says. "Besides, you scooped Beau up; now I'm going to have to lower my standards." He tilts his head and directs his attention to the blond at Payne's side. "Unless you're looking to up yours."

Ah, looks like shit-stirring Griff has come out to play. I snort into my beer at how fast Payne pulls Beau against his side. He has nothing to worry about, but it's cute he thinks he does.

"Leave the loved-up couple alone," Orson says. I don't know much about the guy, but Griff really likes him. If he wasn't straight, I probably would have tried to set them up.

"They're only loved up because of us," Griff says. "They could at least thank me with a threesome."

"Ignoring *that* part." Orson's eyes go wide. "But you have a point. It took Payne way too long to catch on."

Payne scoffs. "I had only just left my ex."

"What would Art say?" Orson says, stroking his gray-streaked scruff. "Time means nothing to love."

"Wow." Beau speaks up. "You all really do drink the Kool-Aid around here, don't you?"

"Art mixes it with his beer," I say.

"Then makes us drink it as part of our DMC initiation," Payne adds.

I nudge Griff. "Have you been officially initiated yet?"

"Not technically. Maybe that's my problem. I need some of Art's special juice to turn into a no-fucks-to-give man-whore."

"Not a man-whore," Payne says, lifting his hand.

Orson gags. "And dear god, man. Never mention Art's *special juices* again. Ever."

"What about my special juices?"

I laugh, because of course Art would show up at the most inappropriate moment. His presence is like a ten-foot radius of unwavering confidence. Tall and commanding, with a filthy mouth and a reputation as large as his ego.

"Jesus," Griff mutters under his breath. "It was nothing."

"Griff was just saying how he wants to drink your juices," I tease. Because hey. If Griff wants some no-strings sex, Art would be the perfect place to start. He's the walking definition of uncommitted.

"Can't blame him," Art says. "Everyone wants the bull juice, but you'll have to get in line, brother. My next few weekends are already full."

Griff's eyes widen. "First, everyone needs to stop saying juices—"

"*Juices,*" I say.

"You started it," Orson points out.

"*Second,* no thanks, Art. Awkward doesn't do it for me. And third, how do you find people? Like, is it an app, or people who come here, or ..."

Art shrugs. "All of the above. We're in tourist season—you couldn't have picked a better time to be single. And with Halloween coming up, this entire place will be full of new blood. And you're in a prime position. You own the place most people stay at—if you can't find some hot hookups with your guests, I'm going to seriously question your game."

Griff looks scandalized. "I can't hook up with guests."

"Why?" I lift my beer to try and hide my smile. "I have."

"You *what?*"

"I'm the guest relations liaison." I wink at him. "It's all there in the title."

Griff groans, probably hoping I'm joking. I'm not. But at least I've never had sex *at* work. I've always taken my hookups back to my place, because I have *some* standards, thanks.

I miss the days of limited responsibility.

With Griff surrounded by friends, I use this moment to fade into the background again. I chat with some of the guys I invited from the gym, tallying in my head who would be a good match for Griff, and then move on to chat with my friend Leif. His partner is a member of the Divorced Men's Club too, and goddamn the pining between the two of them killed my brain. Thank fuck they got their shit together and started dating.

We make small talk for a couple of minutes before I do a quick scan for Griff again and find him missing.

Shit.

There's a fifty-fifty chance he's left. Which means a fifty-fifty chance I'm going to have to yell at myself for taking my eyes off him.

I excuse myself to go and see if I can find him. There's a high chance he only needed a break from it all, so I check the bathroom first, then duck down the hall that leads to Art's office. When I peek into the dark room and find Griff's silhouette in front of the large window, I breathe out a sigh of relief.

I close the door quietly behind me and join him. Neither of us says anything for a moment, even though he knows I'm there.

"Do you remember in high school, when we said we were going to go to college and get a place together and then have the most wild time?"

I squint, trying to pinpoint *which* time. We always used to lie in the back field at his place and talk about what the future would be: how we'd always hang out and nothing would change. It's comforting to think we were almost right. Being around him settles me.

"Sort of. What's your point?"

He tilts his head to look at me, and he's wearing a proper smile for the first time all night. "We're about twenty-five years too late, but this is our chance."

"You wanna move in together?"

His smile is replaced with confusion. "No, I mean the

wild time. I'm scared and nervous and all that, but you're always going on dates, Art is always picking up ... I'm not terrible-looking, right? So I'm trying to convince myself I can have that too."

"Of course you can."

Griff might not be the type of guy I'm drawn toward, but he's hot. Physically big with ripped arms that I like to feel on occasion, paired with vulnerable eyes and a usually relaxed nature.

"Getting sentimental on me?" I ask.

He grunts, then throws my words back at me. "Can you really pretend to be surprised at this point?"

"I don't think anything you do could surprise me."

"Ah, well, I'll keep that in mind."

I laugh softly. "You'll be okay, you know?"

"Yeah, I do. You know I'm crap with adjusting though."

"You are." I rub his back. "You've gotta relax a little."

"That is the plan moving forward. Sure, most of what I'm feeling is too big to deal with right now, but there's excitement there too."

"Good. We'll get you adjusted, and then once you get used to being single, you'll have the best time."

He nods. "Of course."

"As long as you don't fall in love with the first person you stick it in."

"Fuck you." Griff ducks his face into his hand briefly, a good sign he's embarrassed. But as far as wives go, he picked a good one, and that's nothing to be embarrassed about.

"I know you were eighteen and had the best fifteen

seconds of your life, so you're forgiven. But moving forward, there will be no emotions. Only sex."

"Only sex," he repeats. And it definitely sounds like he's trying to convince himself. "What if I'm no good at it?"

"I know you and Poppy haven't done it in a while, but it's like riding a bike. Unless you're riding a cock, then it's not like that at all, but I have confidence you'll figure it out."

"I meant switching off the emotion, asshole. The physical stuff I doubt I'll have a problem with—"

"Don't get too ahead of yourself. You might have women down pat, but sucking cock is an art form."

"If I can find the G-spot, I can manage anything."

"You sweet man. The G-spot is a total myth."

He splutters. "Is not!"

"Well, then I guess you'll have no problem finding it again. And again. Over and over on different women."

His face falls, and he runs a large hand through his hair.

"You okay?"

"In over my head again."

I relent and pull him into a tight hug. His large body sinks against mine, forehead to my shoulder and back moving under his steady breaths. We stand like that for a while. Holding each other, stealing and giving strength in equal measure.

"You know I'm not letting you do this alone," I say. "You were there for me the last few months after Dad ... you know."

He squeezes me tighter. "You still doing okay?"

"Yeah, worried about Mom mostly."

"You're the best son." His hands track slowly up my back and then down again. "And best friend. I'd be lost if I didn't have you."

"I know you would be." I pull back and play punch his jaw, breaking up the serious. "Now, stop focusing on the change; we'll work through things one step at a time."

His smirk is a welcome sight. "You gonna hold my hand through all my hookups as well?"

"If that's your kink, I could be on board. You know there's more fun in numbers."

He laughs and steps away. "That's not something I know at all."

"But you will." I inject as much confidence as I can into my voice. "This is Griff two point oh. Time to get wild."

"Careful, you're starting to sound like Art."

"Damn, that juice is strong."

Griff pretends to cringe, and it's a relief to see him loosening up. We're always like that together—nothing can get us down for long, and I'm dying to have the chilled-out Griff I've always known back. The guy with easy smiles and a calming presence. I meant what I said about being here for him, and I know it's what's helping ease his mind, but what I don't know is how much time I have to give. If I end up getting that job and moving closer to be with Mom, what then?

I promised Griff I'd be here to help him through this.

I'm not sure if I can keep that promise.

Chapter Four

GRIFF

Behind the reception building, surrounded by high gardens, is my new home. We've always used the cottage for storage or overflow accommodation in the summer, and even with my measly belongings filling the space, it still feels so ... impersonal.

They say you're supposed to have life worked out by my age. That things will be smooth sailing. All I know is I'm inheriting a hell of a lot more responsibility and losing the person who's always shared it with me.

Wow. I didn't realize I thought of Poppy that way. Not as my wife or the woman I love, but as someone to help shoulder the workload. I guess next time I wonder if we're doing the right thing, that should give me my answer.

I puff out a breath and look around at the space. It's taken me way too long to finish moving, considering how bare the cottage is. I've got the leather couch and TV from our den, a new oven to replace the worn-out one that was in here, and I've replaced the mattress on the bed but kept the original frame that's always been here.

Still, I'm determined to try and be more positive about everything. Instead of focusing on the drab insides, I turn to the window and look out at my courtyard. It's my pride and joy. The gardens around here have thrived since I started looking after them. I've filled the grounds of the motel with different types of perennials, most of which are in full flower at the moment, and the sight gives me an instant boost.

It's a way better view to wake up to than a sleepy residential street.

I walk out onto my porch, wishing I'd thought to buy something to sit on out here. Even in summer, it gets a cool breeze, and when it comes to being inside or out, nature will always win.

It's still early, which means Michelle or Liarna will be covering the office. Heath doesn't normally arrive until eight, and I don't want to discuss Poppy leaving with the others when I haven't mentioned it to him yet. Especially since, if it came down to a choice between me or her, all three of them would pick her to stay. She's important to the business. Everything I do can be hired out.

Again, not a thought I should be focused on.

I will be positive, dammit. This is a fresh start, and hard to wrap my head around it or not, I'm going to make the most of it.

No more plodding along.

Our property is right at the base of the Provin Mountain, on the outskirts of town and only five minutes' walk from the main tourist hub. The old Kilborough Penitentiary —Kill Pen for short—looms overhead and is the reason we do such good business. The prison grounds and surrounding ghost town were abandoned sometime in the seventies when the prison closed down and jobs around here dried up. But in the last twenty or so years, Kilborough has exploded with the reopening of the prison as a historical site and the city embracing the theme of catering to all things spooky.

The grass is damp as I walk a lap of the property, taking in what my hard work has built. The reception building is the first thing you see when you come down the drive and is separate from the main part of the resort. Most of our rooms are in one giant U-shaped building. They're small and comfortable with private courtyards out of sight of reception, and then we have the cabins dotted across the property with different views of the mountains. Seeing this place transform from a seedy old motel to what it is now is a constant reminder that I've done something big with my life.

I cross the grounds to the woods lining our property and follow a familiar path. The smell of fresh air and rotting foliage is calming, and I zone out as I walk. I love this place. It's always given me that extra boost when I needed it, which is part of the reason I chose to move in here. Magnolia Ridge isn't a huge business, but the staff are all our family, and the business, the grounds, the gardens I've worked so hard on …

I have no idea how Poppy is moving on when I don't think I ever could.

The frustration and helplessness bleeds out of my soul the farther I walk. These woods lead to an area farther down that is being cleared to make way for a new development.

That thought makes me pause. If they haven't finished clearing the land, I'll have my pick of lumber that I can take off their hands and turn into furniture. While Poppy loved my *hobby*, as she called it, we were never on the same page about furniture for the house, so I haven't created much of anything lately.

She likes modern, ugly glass and metal things. My taste leans toward wood and greenery. Warmth. A home that makes me feel relaxed and not like I'm going to break the table by setting my mug on it.

The thought of being able to shape wood into something I can use buoys me. It's another silver lining.

And when I get to the development, I'm in luck. A lot of the trees have already been removed, but there are still large stumps ringing the outskirts and some trunks they haven't hauled off yet.

Technically, I'm not supposed to be down here.

Like that's gonna stop me.

And even though I'm reluctant to walk away empty-handed, the workers are already showing up for the day, so I'll have to come back tonight when no one is around.

By the time I'm back home, Heath is already there, making himself coffee in my kitchen. I guess it doesn't matter where I live; he'll always be a permanent fixture in my life. I have no idea what I did to deserve him as a best friend, but I thank my lucky stars every day.

"Why are bachelor pads depressingly empty?" I ask Heath as he lifts a cup to me, asking if I want one. I shake my head.

"It's called minimalist," he answers. "It's a style, man."

I look around again, realizing that I don't miss the books and art Poppy filled the house with. "I guess I can make it work."

"Of course you can." He narrows his eyes as he looks around again. "But I'm, uh, gonna bring some more things around. You at least need a table and chairs."

"Why?"

"Because I want somewhere to sit when I come over."

"Right. And my house obviously must cater to your needs."

"Duh." He jumps up to sit on the short counter.

"Well, you can quit your whining. I'm going down to that new development tonight to grab some wood to make a couple of chairs."

His eyebrows shoot up. "You're going to build again?"

"Might as well."

"Nice." He smiles. "My Griff will be back in no time."

I shift and swipe at my face in an attempt to hide the way my cheeks heat at the compliment. "It's nothing. Just a hobby."

"A hobby you're damn good at. Embrace your talent, man."

"Calm down, it's been years. Knowing my luck, I'll cut my hand off before I even get started."

"Then you really will be a *handy* man."

I flip him off.

Heath laughs, then drains his mug and hops down off the counter. "You working today or still have some time off?"

"I'm not supposed to be back until Monday."

"Excellent. I can continue to play king."

That reminds me of something he said last night. "Please don't hit on the guests."

"Can't make any promises."

"Heath ..."

"What?" He holds up his hands. "Some of the guys staying here are really fucking hot."

"I'm sure they are, but ..." I guess I probably need to tell him sooner than later. "I'm, uh, probably going to need you to help me out around here."

Heath's brown eyes flick over me, trying to read the reason before I can tell him. "Ah ... why?"

"Well, turns out Poppy wasn't just getting rid of me but the business as well."

He takes a minute to turn that over in his head. "She's leaving?"

"Still unclear on the details, but she doesn't want to run things anymore."

"And, what? You're taking over?"

I crack a smile. "No need to sound so judgmental about it."

"Sorry, but do you even know how to turn a computer on?"

"I can turn it *on*." I run a hand through my hair. "Just don't know what to do with it once I get it there."

To his credit, he doesn't laugh at me, even though I know he really, really wants to. "Okay, so we'll need to teach you the booking system, and the accounting software, and how to run the social media accounts ..."

I can feel my eyes growing wider by the second.

"Griff ..."

I barely know what he's talking about, let alone how to do any of these things. Some false confidence would be welcome right now. I'd been right in that the motel would be a good investment, and when we bought it as a total dump, I fixed it up almost by myself. Heath pitched in, and I had trades come in for the things I couldn't do, but all the elbow grease was me. When it came to actually opening the place though, Poppy took over the books and day-to-day operations.

I force a smile. "I'll figure it out."

"You will."

"Thank fuck I'll have you here to help me though."

For some reason, he hesitates. "Of course you will."

"Thank you." I mean it.

"It'll be too easy."

"Until after you realize how much extra work it'll be."

Heath chuckles. "Out of the two of us, I don't think *I'm* the one who's going to be caught unprepared."

"True." Way to remind me I'm in way over my head. "I appreciate it."

"I know. I'm a lifesaver. You're completely blessed to have me in your life."

"Don't you have work to be doing?" I ask.

"Wow. You couldn't even be subtle about wanting to get rid of me, huh?" He turns and heads for the door.

"Drinks tonight?" I ask.

"I thought you were planning on raiding Mother Nature."

Shit, I was. "Okay, why don't you help me do the heavy lifting, and then we'll have drinks after?"

"You're going to make me earn my reward through heavy labor? Geez, you really are a hard-ass."

"Fine. No rewards for you if you're going to be an asshole about it."

"I'm not being an asshole."

"All you had to do was say *thanks, Griff, sounds great.* It almost sounds like you don't want to hang out with me."

"It almost sounds like someone's lonely and doesn't want to be here solo tonight."

"Fuck off."

"Aww, is my widdle Griffy in need of company?"

"Someone's on their patronizing A game." I cross my arms. "Can't help but notice you also haven't given me an answer, so I'm going to take that as a no."

"No, it's ..." He hesitates. I watch him rub his jaw as he stares across the room. Then he suddenly nods. "Sounds good."

"Riiight." I eye him, because that definitely wasn't usual Heath behavior. "Everything okay?"

"Sure is. Just calculating how many guests I can pick up today."

"Get out."

He leaves, laughing as he goes, but I can't shake the feeling that something was off with that conversation.

Chapter Five

HEATH

Poppy's leaving. If I'm honest, there was always a part of me that thought one of them would go, but I'd assumed it would be Griff. I love my best friend, and as much as he loves chatting with the guests and helping with the big picture running of the place, he's never been in control of any of it.

Michelle looks half asleep when I take over for her in the office, and even though the overnight shifts tend to be slower than during the day, we're in the middle of our busy season with full occupancy for months straight. We all pray for Halloween, because after October, things drop right off.

I love working here. Every day is varied; I know what I'm doing, and I enjoy the work, plus the staff are fantastic people. Every time I confirm a room is ready before check-in and leave a handwritten welcome card, every time I pass through the arches of honeysuckle or the paths lined with lavender, every time I see Griff laughing with someone or hauling deliveries into the restaurant or up on a ladder doing fuck knows what, this sense of peace washes over me.

I don't want to lose any of it.

Thanks to my initiative over the last few years, I can run this place with my eyes closed, which is lucky since apparently I'm going to have to do exactly that.

My heart sinks when I consider that even if I *am* offered this other job, I probably won't take it. I never specifically *wanted* out in the first place—the job was a way for me to be close to Mom, but I'd be lying if I said I wasn't scrambling to find a reason to stay. I almost wish I didn't make that promise to Dad.

I blame Griff, mostly.

He's always been a crutch for me. Even when he got loved up with Poppy, we stayed close. I'm godfather to Felix, and when they floated the idea of buying this place, there was never any question about whether I'd be in.

I sigh as my conversation with Griff this morning comes back to me. He has no idea what he's getting himself into, and it's not that he's stupid—because he isn't—but he's also not made for office work. Thinking of him sitting at this computer all day ... it won't happen. And if I don't step up, this place will be run into the ground, and we'll all end up with nothing.

That thought is another reminder that as much as I view this place as mine and the people who work here as my own little community, that's not the case at all.

I'm an employee, same as everyone else.

There could definitely be worse things.

Like the state of Griff's depressing new home. He might not see it yet, but this is the move that's going to catapult him back into the man I know—aaand great. Now I sound like Art.

Thankfully my day is jam-packed, thanks to Poppy and Griff's absence, so it passes quickly, and by the time five o'clock comes around, I do one more lap of the grounds to make sure everything is fine. The tennis court and pool will be locked up later, but for now, I'm fine to head off. And I don't have to walk far.

On the way to Griff's, I take a detour through the gardens to pick a handful of flowers for him. He's not a *flowers* guy per se, but Griff has always loved nature and gotten a boost from it. The number of times I've had to hear him mutter about the fake plants Poppy filled their house with was ridiculous, and since I know he's having a hard time at the moment, I'm hoping the extra color inside will give him a boost.

I don't bother to knock when I get there, and I walk in to find Griff lying on the couch, hands behind his head, looking sleepy and relaxed. It's one of my favorite versions of him, the kind that comes with a deep contentment that I haven't seen for a long time.

His gaze snags on the flowers as I walk into his kitchen and hunt for something to put them in.

"No vase," I say. "Should have figured."

"You brought me flowers?"

"Don't get too excited, big guy. They're your flowers. I just brought them inside for you."

He laughs, pushing up to sit. "Thank you."

"Whatever you need, bestie." Settling on a glass, I fill it with water and dump the flowers inside. "And now what *I* need is to borrow some of your sexy, sexy clothes." I wink and head for his bedroom, mentally preparing myself for the oh-so-sexy feel of denim and flannel. *Gag.* I dunno what Griff finds comforting about dressing like a hobo, but he's lucky I love him anyway.

He sniggers as soon as I leave his room. "How do you still manage to look like a city boy in my clothes?"

"It's a gift." And since there's still nowhere for me to sit, I round the couch and pull him to his feet. "Let's go get you some wood and get back here."

He groans, and I realize my mistake a second too late. "You can't talk about wood when it's been forever since I've gotten laid."

Me too, man. Not that anyone knows that. "You've been single for a few nights now—seems like a you problem if you haven't fixed it by now."

"Still getting the courage together." He pauses. "You're coming out this weekend, right?"

"Of course." My boy needs sex, and I'm going to be his wingman.

After a quick beer at his kitchen counter, we head out. Griff throws on a denim jacket with no shirt, and when I throw a skeptical look in his direction, he says, "It's hot, but I don't want to get splinters."

In his shoulders, maybe. I'm not risking getting them in my nipples.

We take shovels and axes with us, and while I'm hopeless at things like this, I do my best to help out. Not that Griff needs it.

This is where he dominates. He's efficient, confident, and makes quick work of tearing two large tree stumps from the ground. He brings part of the root system up, dirt clinging to the twisted tendrils.

With a grunt, Griff ducks down and hauls one of them up onto his shoulder.

"Show-off." But even I can admit the show of strength is a hot look.

I swing my axe a few times and cut my stump into more manageable pieces, then follow Griff back, taking the opportunity to check out the way his jeans stretch obscenely over his full ass.

We make a few trips between his place and the development before Griff is satisfied we have enough wood. I'd feel guilty for the whole, you know, *stealing* thing if it was for anyone but him. I'm excited over the idea of him creating again. And I have complete confidence he won't cut off his hand.

Probably.

Griff dumps his final haul onto the pile and lets out a long breath. We're both sweaty, and my hands feel raw, but even as I unbutton my shirt to take it off, Griff shrugs out of his denim jacket and ...

Well, hellooo, big guy.

I've seen him nearly naked plenty of times, but there's something about the combination of sweat and shadows, the light shining from his living room behind him, that makes me forget it's Griff. Plus, the way he's relaxed and happy like he hasn't been in a long time is really fucking ... attractive. All my brain is able to focus on is those nommy nommy muscles.

Normally muscles don't do much for me, but for some reason, my blood is heating up.

"I think we both seriously need to get laid," I say.

"Agreed, but that was random."

"I'm terrifyingly attracted to you right now," I tell him. "Something is wrong with me."

Griff bursts out laughing. "Come on, it's been ... a week or two for you? Try going as long as me, and then you can complain." He presses down on his cock. "I swear it takes nothing for me to get it up these days."

My gaze trails along his ripped arms to where the bulge in his pants seems to be getting larger. It's hard to tell in this lighting, so it could definitely be my imagination, but I'm going to lean into the image.

"Heath, shit. Cut it out."

I pull my attention back up to meet his. Griff doesn't look so amused anymore. And the longer we stand there looking at each other, the weirder this whole thing is getting. "Horny?" I ask.

"So horny I'd even do you."

"Pity I have standards."

"I've seen some of the men you've slept with, and I disagree," he says.

That breaks the tension between us. "Oh, I don't mean looks." Because while twinkish dudes are my type, I'm not picky. "But you are a stage-five clinger, man, and that's so not my style."

He grimaces, and like that, I can tell he's starting to over-think again. "I am, aren't I?"

"What? No, it was a joke."

"Then what else do you call sleeping with someone and spending the next twenty-five years with them?"

"That's not happening this time. I won't let it."

"You might be fighting a losing battle."

I grin and drop down to sit on the side of the porch. "You're forgetting that I like a challenge."

"Yes, but at least with a challenge, you have the chance to win. I think I'm a lost cause."

"Nah, no way. You just need ... guidance. Some no-strings rules."

His long, measured strides shouldn't catch my attention the way they do, but I watch him right up until he's sitting next to me. The smell of his sweat invades my nostrils, making it harder to shake the images of sex.

"Rules?"

"Ah ..." Come on, brain, get back online. "Rules, yeah. Some noncommitment rules that you can follow to make sure you don't fall into feelings again."

"Okay. Like what?"

"We'll start with baby steps. A club for your first hookup

is a good move. No names. No personal details. There'll be loud music, so even if you wanted to ask questions, you wouldn't hear the answers anyway. And no going home with anyone either. A quick bathroom hookup, then you'll get out. No small talk."

He's nodding, and I spare a quick glance his way to find him frowning.

"Does that sound okay?" I ask.

"No, but I probably need to get it out of the way, don't I?"

"It might help. Then again, I'm no expert."

"And a club ... that won't be weird?"

"Why?"

"You know." He waves a hand over himself. "Aren't they for young people?"

"Not where I go." Or where I used to go. Since Dad died, I haven't felt up to the party scene.

Griff shifts in place, rubbing his arm and staring out into the dark courtyard. "I'm so out of my element, Heath."

"You don't have to do anything you're not comfortable with," I remind him.

"I know ..." He glances at me, then quickly away again, before reaching over and giving my ear a tug. Warmth blooms in my gut. It's an old, familiar gesture. One we don't use often anymore. One I didn't realize until now that I've missed.

Neither one of us was big with affection when we were younger, especially in front of people, so we decided if we needed a hug or a moment, we'd tug on the other's ear. It looks playful to most people, but to us, it meant so much more.

And since no one else is around, I don't hesitate to wrap an arm around his shoulders and pull him close enough to plant a kiss on the top of his head.

"You'll be okay, Griff."

"I know I will." He sounds the most confident I've heard since I picked him up from the airport. "I have you."

DMC Group Chat

Griff: *I'm building again.*

Orson*: Way to go, man. I'm so happy for you.*

Art: *Literally building, or rebuilding your life from the ashes of your marriage, like a Phoenix bursting from flame?*

Payne: *... times like these, I really do think he's messing with us.*

Art: *What?*

Payne: *Phoenix? FLAME?! Come on ...*

Orson: *If you're done bickering, can we go back to being supportive?*

Art: *I'm always supportive. It's basically my middle name.*

Griff: *I thought your middle name was horny?*

Art: *Artur Solidário O Caralho de Almeida.*

Payne: *Supportive dick? Yep. He's fucking with us.*

Art: *Vão se foder. I'm delightful.*

Griff: *Delightfully messed up maybe.*

Chapter Six

GRIFF

I swear every day that passes is like some kind of weird fever dream. And yet ... it's starting to feel good.

I'm still shitting myself, don't get me wrong, but it's sinking in that for the first time in ... ever, I'm not accountable to anyone but me. I don't have to justify my comings and goings, and I don't have to consider someone else in my decisions.

That's both exhilarating and terrifying, but I'm choosing to lean into the former.

Heath and I are going out tomorrow, and it's so, so tempting to message Poppy and give her the heads-up. She's not home until Monday though, and I'm slowly rewiring my brain to remove her from my life.

I drain my mug and set it in the sink, getting a low level of satisfaction out of not rinsing it right away. It's one of the many small things I've been doing to remind myself that I don't have to report to anyone. I wear shoes in the house and set my jacket over the back of the couch. Maybe the hardest thing I'm still learning to do is sleep in the center of the bed. It feels ... unnatural. But dammit, I'm going to succeed there too.

While every day this week has been a lesson in pushing my singledom, they've been baby steps, and if I'm going to hook up with a complete random tomorrow, I want to take a big leap today.

My hand runs over the hair on my chest as I look out the window, lost in thought. My pile of wood and shavings are right outside, but I still need to go and buy the tools to properly get started on building anything worth using. I've been messing around, happy to get used to the feel of wood again.

Speaking of wood ...

I look down at my cock pressing against the inside of my briefs. Whoever said my sex drive would die down as I got older severely underestimated the effect an extended dry spell would have on me.

I've jerked off as much as I ever have this week, but it's only now occurring to me that I've still been sticking to the shower as a means of getting off.

Now I'm single and have my own place ... why is anywhere off-limits?

I'm equal parts nervous and excited as I push my briefs down and kick them off. The entire house is bright from the morning sun flooding through the open windows, but even though I know no one comes around here, a thrill runs down my spine anyway.

I spit into my hand and wrap it around my rapidly hardening cock. Maybe I'll make a habit of this, jerking off in every room in the house. It's my place now. My rules.

My head drops back on a soft moan as I let that thought take hold. Whenever and wherever I want.

I stroke myself, slowly at first, a tease of foreskin sliding up and down my shaft. I've wanted to invest in a Fleshlight for a while now, so maybe I'll buy one of those too. Hell, maybe even a dildo. Some anal beads ...

I curse at not having lube on hand as my ass twitches, begging for me to shove a finger in there. But with how fast I'm getting turned on, there's no way I'm going to risk stopping to grab some and wind up ruining my high.

My grip tightens, and I plant my feet wider to reach my balls instead. I pull and tug on them as I fuck into my fist, loving the delicious ache I'm working up, even as I stare out my window at the courtyard.

If someone walked in there ... one look at me and they'd know. They'd know I'm pleasuring myself in my kitchen, touching my cock, and getting harder and needier by the second. Random images fly through my mind of boobs and pussy and rock-hard cocks. A slideshow of scenes from various pornos I've watched plays on a loop in my mind.

My gaze drops to my porch, remembering the other night when Heath hugged me to him. His strong arms around me. Him eyeing me shirtless, dark gaze dropping to my groin. The way his tongue swiped over his lips in a way he didn't notice he was doing.

A satisfied hum starts in my chest and gets louder the longer I focus on that moment between us. The moment I'm almost positive I could have gotten sex if either of us actually wanted to go there.

And the thought of Heath should be a turnoff, but given the throb of my cock, that's not what's happening here. So I let the image play out. Morph into less of a reality and more of a fantasy.

Him stalking closer, sinking to his knees, removing my hand from my cock and replacing it with his own.

"Fuck, yes ..."

My balls have tightened to the point I can barely get a grip on them anymore, and the images in my head are starting to flick in and out of focus. All I can concentrate on is how hard I am, how desperate. The steady *fap, fap, fap* gets faster. I let my balls go and place my hand on the counter to steady myself as I pound into my fist. Heath's mouth, Heath's tongue, Heath's confident smirk as he leans forward and swallows me down.

I'm close. Throbbing. Reaching that high that only ever comes from a top-tier orgasm, right on the edge, needing one ... more ...

"*Nrgh.*" I bite down into my lip on reflex as I finally unleash. I shoot hard, over and over, until the shivery pleasure ebbs and a little sanity returns.

I wait for the loneliness to kick in, like it so often has been lately, but instead, the opposite happens. A burst of freedom balloons in my chest, drawing out the aftereffects of sex.

The only thing I'm unsettled over is picturing Heath to get myself off. That was ... uncalled for.

Maybe I need to come up with some rules of my own. Ways to keep our friendship intact and to stop my dick from blurring lines it has no business blurring.

I shake off the weirdness, then take a moment to wipe everything down and wash my hands. Just as I'm turning the tap off, my front door opens and Heath walks in.

God fucking dammit.

"Morning," he says, eyes trained on his phone.

I freeze, glancing over to where I've kicked my briefs and weighing up my chances of grabbing them and pulling them on before he sees.

Unfortunately, Heath makes straight for me, dumping the handful of flowers he's carrying on the counter and rounding it to join me in the kitchen. I don't have time to move, and when he walks in, it's obvious the moment his gaze slips from his phone and lands on my underwear.

He pauses, then slowly looks up at me. Finding me buck naked makes his smile spring to life. "Well, good morning, hot stuff."

I flip him off.

"Geez, if I'd known you were serving up breakfast, I would have waited."

"Coffee?" I ask, ignoring him. I turn to grab a cup, hoping if I ignore that I'm naked, he will too.

"Of course. You know I like caffeine and a view."

"You're not going to let this drop, are you?" He doesn't answer, but I hear him hop up onto the counter, and I glance over my shoulder to catch him checking out my ass. "Do you mind?"

"Not at all. Carry on."

Ah, fuck it. Not like we haven't seen each other naked before.

But have you seen him naked right after thinking about him while you jerked off?

Urg, that's not helpful. And now I can't turn around and face him because my cheeks are flaming hot. Damn pale skin.

"Embarrassed?" he asks.

Well, keeping my back to him didn't work. "Picked up on that, did you?"

"I can read you like a book."

He can too. It'd be irritating if I couldn't do it right back to him. I pour his coffee, then turn and hand it over.

"Thanks." He takes a long sip, eyes falling closed, and lets me think for a whole couple of seconds that he's letting me off the hook. Until he opens his mouth again. "You know, I'm always teasing you about your flannel shirts, but it wasn't a choice between them and nothing. Because while *I* approve, other people might be scandalized."

It's times like these I wish Heath wasn't so forward. While I know for a fact his interest isn't anything more than surface-level appreciation, I'm so hard up for sex that my body is struggling to differentiate between something fake and something real.

Thank fuck I jerked off, or I'd have an awkward boner issue on top of all the naked.

I'm determined not to get embarrassed over this though. "Thought I'd try something new."

"A little breeze on your balls?"

"Exactly. They've been neglected for way too long."

"Tomorrow night, that all changes."

I nod, even as the familiar apprehension tries to take hold. It's irritating. I *want* to hook up. It's more that I'm not sure if I can go through with it.

"Stop," Heath says. "I can see you thinking again."

"It'll be fine. I know that. I think I need to rip the bandage off so I'm not building it up into a bigger thing than it is."

"Exactly." He cocks his head, gaze back on my body.

"You done yet?"

"Not quite. You know, I don't think I've ever given you enough credit, Griff."

"What do you mean?"

"Well, when did you get so hot?"

And dammit, there go my cheeks again. "Screw it, I'm putting on clothes."

He laughs. "Relax, I'm leaving in a minute. If you want to do some bare-ass exhibitionism thing to scare all the guests, that's on you."

"You know nobody comes out this way."

"You *hope*." His gaze runs back down to my cock. "You jerked off, didn't you?"

"*What?*"

He gestures to it. "That's a happy kitty you've got there."

"Happy kitty?"

"Mhmm. That thing is practically purring. You must have pet it real good."

I take his almost empty mug from him and place it in the sink beside mine. "Time to go. It's not even eight and we're already approaching creepy territory."

"Approaching? Man, we were there when I walked in to find you in your birthday suit. And if my opinion counts for anything, this is on Heath's approved list of attire, by the way."

And because I know he's only trying to get under my skin, I decide to play his game right back.

I stalk over to him, catching him by surprise when I push open his legs and step between them.

His thighs brush my hips, and while this is supposed to be me teasing him, it's also the closest I've been to someone like this in a really, really long time.

"Careful, buddy," I say. "It's been a lifetime for me, and if you keep going, my body isn't going to recognize that the flirting is all bullshit."

Heath's eyes flick up and meet mine. "Maybe you're the one who should be careful." He leans in, and that familiar sweet cologne surrounds me. "Because I don't think your flirting is bullshit at all."

Then he pointedly looks down to where I'm starting to chub up again.

Yep. Time to get those platonic rules in place.

Number one apparently needs to be no getting hard over Heath.

The whole thing is so ridiculous I laugh.

"I think you might be right." I force a step back away from him. "Sorry. I swear I'll be less of a horndog once I get some goddamn action."

"I don't think either of us believes that. For someone who loves sex so much, I am in complete shock how long you've held off."

I shrug. "You know I wouldn't hurt Felix or Poppy for anything."

"I know." He climbs off the counter, and I watch every movement of his long, lean body.

"You really need to go though," I say. "Because I'm worried what might happen if you stay."

"I *am* pretty hot."

"Nope. I'm just *that* desperate."

"Touché." Heath grabs his phone, and when he passes me, he whacks my ass so hard I swear my cheek goes numb. "Nice ass, bestie."

"I hate you."

Chapter Seven

HEATH

I am the ultimate professional. Even as a kid, I was always that bit more responsible than the rest of my peers. I'm not a risk taker; I don't even want to be one. I thrive off to-do lists and organization and keeping life simple.

It's why most of the time I prefer hookups over relationships—not that I'm against them—but when you're with someone, there's a far greater likelihood that you'll end up breaking up, and I hate the heartache and bitterness that goes along with it.

Hooking up casually works. Both sides know the score, and I'm never left with regrets or complications.

And now ... now I can't stop thinking about Griff naked. If that isn't a complication, I don't know what is. Not only is he my best friend, but he's technically my boss too, even though he'd never pull that shit with me. I shouldn't be thinking about him this way. It's not something I've ever really done before, and I say "really" because during a mess of teenage hormones, I'd mooned after him for about a week before moving on to my next crush.

Since then, never.

Maybe it's because he's always been off-limits. From the moment he hooked up with Poppy, I could tell she wasn't going anywhere, and it's lucky we got along so well, or I might not be here now.

But even with how right they were for each other, the cracks have been showing for a while. The fighting, resentment, and tension were impossible to miss, but ever since they agreed to split, the status quo resumed.

You know, if you forget the fact Poppy is moving on, Griff is living at work, and my best friend has turned into a sex-crazed maniac.

The image of his flushed face from this morning comes back to me again. It was easy enough to guess that he'd been jerking off, given the state I'd found him in. And while I saw his dick a lot when we were younger, he has grown up a lot since then. But it wasn't even his dick. He looked like—I don't even know.

Fucking ... radiant? I think that's the word. I'd almost swallowed my tongue at how open and relaxed he was.

I squeeze my eyes closed and remind myself *professional, I am a professional.*

Just because Griff is suddenly single does *not* mean I need to go there. Us being available and sex deprived at the same time probably isn't a great thing, so while tomorrow is about getting him laid, I think I'm going to have to sort myself out too.

"Heath, can you come here for a moment?" Jody calls from the reception desk.

I close out of the payroll system, glad to have a distraction. Anything, *anything* is welcome if it means keeping my mind off Griff and his body.

"What's up?"

"I think we have a problem. Thirteen doesn't check out until Monday, but the next guests are booked in from Sunday."

Of course they are.

I nod to prevent myself from doing something stupid like swearing.

I've made it through the past two weeks without having to deal with any double bookings, so of course the day before Griff and Poppy are due to return to work, one pops up. Glitch or staff error, who knows, but it does have to be resolved.

Which will not be an easy thing when we're still in peak holiday season and most places are booked out.

I refuse to look frustrated in front of Jody though.

"I'm on it. Think you can do a quick walk around for me?"

"Of course."

She leaves, and I let out a long breath. Disappointing people is not something I do lightly. It always leaves me feeling vaguely sick and out of control.

First step is calling to confirm all of our reservations, and of course I can't hit luck and have someone cancel, because that would make things too easy for me. Normally, this is where we'd set up the back cabin and pass it off as an upgrade, but with Griff living there now, my options are limited.

Who around here offers a similar level of accommodation and actually has rooms free?

Short answer? No one.

Nowhere in Kilborough is like Magnolia Ridge.

I groan and scrub a hand through my hair, hoping to loosen up my thoughts and come up with ... something.

My phone dings beside me, and a quick glance at the display shows Griff's name. I'm tempted to reply so I can try to pass this off to him, but unlike Poppy, he'll have less idea how to handle this than I do.

Nope. I'm on my own with it.

He sends another text, so I give in and check them.

Griff: *Are my grays too much? Should I dye my hair or whatever? What's the etiquette here?*

Me: *Relax. Grays are fine. Everyone likes a Daddy.*

Griff: *Dyeing it, it is.*

Me: *I'm joking—like you could pull off a Daddy. Well, literally, you could probably PULL one off, given how much practice you've had jerking off these days.*

Griff: *Never going to let me live that down, are you?*

Me: *Are you kidding? I've burned this morning into my memory forever.*

Griff: *Good to know. So dyeing my hair is a yes, next item for discussion: pubes. Bush, trimmed, or bare?*

And like that, I'm thinking of him naked again.

Me: *Lucky for you, I got a good look this morning and am totally capable of speaking from experience in this area. While you make the bush work, my preference is trimmed. Less chance of a pube to the throat when you're giving head, and it makes your cock look bigger.*

Griff: *We both know I don't need help in that department.*

Me: *Clearly you don't see a whole lot of dicks.*

Griff: *Fuck you. I watch plenty of porn.*

Me: *Shocking news that you might want to sit down for: porn isn't real.*

Griff: *Great. Just great. So you're telling me I don't measure up. As if I wasn't already anxious enough as it is.*

I burst out laughing, picturing the forehead lines Griff gets whenever he's overwhelmed about something. It's not even lunchtime yet, and I want to ask him to catch up so I can reassure him yet again, but I need to get this double booking fixed, then finish setting up everyone's pays, then make sure everything is organized for the weekend.

I don't have time to slack off, even if I want to.

Me: *I know this is scary, but you've got to take a breath, Griff. I'll come over after work. No dyeing hair until then.*

Griff: *Aww are you going to help me?*

Me: *Only if I can't talk you out of it.*

Griff: *Will you help me shave my balls too?*

Me: *That one you can get started on solo. I'm not going near your junk.*

Griff: *But what if I ... you know. Cuuuut them?*

I cringe over the mere thought of nicking my ball sac.

Me: *Go slow. Be gentle. For the love of your nuts, pay attention.*

Griff: *Got it, coach. Wanna do lunch?*

Me: *I want to, but can't. Little problem here I need to solve, then I have to get everything wrapped up before the weekend so we can switch off work and focus on play.*

Griff: *My best friend is a clever one. Fine. I'll spend some time prettying my dick up and then we can do dinner instead.*

I agree, but it's with a twinge of guilt. A year ago, I would have jumped at the chance for him to be single, for us to go out and party, be each other's wingman in a way we never have been before. I was thrilled to show him around, to teach him how to live up the single life.

Weekends are normally when I drive up to see Mom though, and I need to find a way to support my guy completely while making sure Mom doesn't feel forgotten about. With Dad gone, the last thing I want is for her to feel like she has no one left. She's getting older, and my time with her is valuable and important—losing Dad taught me that. It's what prompted the whole job search. But my time with Griff is important to me too.

I can't even mention the interview to Griff because he's got enough on his plate with learning to run this place, and it would only stress him out more to think of me leaving.

And like that, I remember the overbooking and force everything else from my mind.

I'm only human.

One thing at a time.

No outside stresses. No unexpected sexual tension.

Just me running this place like it's my own.

Even though it isn't.

Chapter Eight

GRIFF

With Heath tied up at work and my dick about a pound lighter from its haircut, I jump in my car and head into town.

I'm more anxious over tomorrow night than I'm going to let on, and while I'd normally go to Art for a pep talk, he's not the one who will understand feeling this way. He fucks around like it's his job—he's the one I go to if I need a kick up the ass and motivation for days.

Orson is the one I chat to when I need actual advice.

And since Heath is busy with work, I'm taking my issues with getting ready to him. Because knowing Art, I'd walk away with a new haircut, clothes, and probably wax in places I've never wanted it to go. Not to mention something would end up pierced.

I shudder at that thought as I pull up in the Killer Brew parking lot. I grab my tea and Orson's usual coffee order from the outside cafe before crossing the street. Orson will be working, but unlike Heath, he won't be run off his feet. At least that's what I assume before I walk into the florists and find a few people browsing the selection.

Orson is ringing an order up behind the counter, but as soon as he sees his coffee, he waves me over.

"Lifesaver." He takes the to-go cup and has a long sip.

"What's going on?" I ask, nodding toward a group of three people discussing a display.

"A twenty-first birthday this weekend. Apparently, flowers are all the birthday girl wants. Her room is going to look like my shop."

I chuckle. "Good for you though, right?"

"I'm not complaining." He leans his hip against the counter, taking advantage of the break in customers. "How's this week been treating you?"

"I told you guys, it's been great."

"Uh-huh. Which is why you're here in the middle of a workday."

"I was bored?"

He eyes me with amusement. "Would it make you feel better if I pretended to believe you?"

"No." I let out a long breath. "I really do want to talk."

I cut off as an older man approaches with a bouquet, and Orson turns to serve him. Orson comes alive when he's interacting with customers, genuinely caring about their

71

stories and relationships, even after losing his. I have no idea how he moved on from what happened.

I feel bad for coming to him with my shit. My breakup was a mutual decision; he didn't have a choice in losing his wife. Even though things are over between Poppy and me, the thought of something happening to her ... I shift at the harsh twist in my gut.

"What did you want to talk about?" Orson asks.

"Heath and I are going out tomorrow night."

A spark of understanding hits his kind eyes. "And you're uncertain how you feel about sleeping with someone else."

"Yep. I can't remember the last time I went to a club, and even though Heath says it will be okay ... I've let myself go in about every way possible."

"What are you talking about?"

I lean in to whisper so his customers don't overhear. "I've just finished ... *manscaping.* Do you know what that is?"

He sniggers. "Everyone knows what that is."

"And have you done it before?"

"That's not information you ever need to know."

I huff a breath. "Well, it's not something I've ever thought about for myself. Even knowing the split was coming, I tried not to go over all the details. I focused on the end goal of being single and enjoying it. Turns out there are a lot of fucking steps I didn't consider."

"Maybe because those steps aren't important."

I bite my thumbnail to hold back a response. I know

what he's thinking—sex is sex. That's what everyone keeps saying. "I'm being stupid."

"Why?"

I shrug. "It's only sex. I get it. It isn't a big deal."

"We both know you don't believe that."

My cheeks heat up. "All dudes do."

"No, they don't." He crosses his arms, drawing my attention to the tiny scars all up and down his forearms. "That's what people want you to think, but neither of us feels that way. Does that mean we're not dudes?"

My lips twitch. "Okay, okay. Use logic against me."

"Gladly."

Our conversation has to pause again when Orson is dragged away to put together a custom bunch for someone. I take the seat behind the counter as I wait for him to finish up.

When he's done, he walks back toward me, wiping his hands off on his apron, pitying stare in place.

"Don't give me that look," I say.

"What I said about the steps not being important ... I wasn't talking about sex. Or trying to minimize what you're going through. All I meant was that you're *already* single, Griff. You can already be enjoying yourself and living it up or whatever; you don't need to sleep with someone for that to happen. Sex isn't the only goal here."

"It just seems like the biggest one."

"I can see that." He runs his fingers over his short beard. The gray patches catch my attention, like they normally do, but for a different reason this time.

"You don't dye your hair."

His forehead crumples. "No ..."

"So does that mean I don't have to dye mine?"

He laughs. "Griff ..." Orson glances around to make sure no one else needs him before grabbing another chair. "This is divorce—no need to add a midlife crisis on top of it as well. If you want to dye your hair, then dye it, but don't do it because you think it'll get you laid. There's no pressure, no one way to be single, which is why I can't tell you what to do. No one can—though we both know Art will try."

"Maybe I should have gone to him."

"No, you made a smart choice coming here. Art's solution would have been to pull out his dick and ask you to blow him." Orson cringes. "Feeling like you *have* to get it over with, like sex is a chore, probably isn't the way to play this."

"New question, then: What did you do? When you finally got back out there?"

He's silent for a moment. "My only advice is to take things slow, wait until you're there and things are happening, then listen to yourself and pay attention to your boundaries."

That is more or less what I've been telling myself, but it's good to hear it come from someone else as well. The problem is, I'm done with waiting. I want the outcome, and I want it happening now.

"I have a question for you," he says.

I tilt my head to show I'm listening.

"Are you sure you're ready for this? You don't *have* to

jump straight into hooking up with people just because you feel like it's what you're expected to do."

"I know." And I do. I'm not a complete idiot. There isn't a rush to any of this beyond the looming need to get it out of the way. "But I think I'm going to stress about it until I get the first one done and dusted."

"And you're ready to have no-strings-attached sex?"

"Yes. Heath and I have rules."

Orson looks like he's struggling against a laugh. "Rules?"

"To stop me from getting attached."

"Like ...?"

No hard-ons for Heath. "No names. No leaving the club. Just a total random hookup with no means of contacting them again."

He looks at me like I'm high. "Well, in that case, you've convinced me. You're totally ready. Nothing can go wrong here."

"Orson ..."

"Hey, if you marry the first person you sleep with, can I be your best man?"

"Serious time is over, then, huh?" I ask.

"I'm not so sure it even began."

Another influx of customers arrive, so I leave Orson to it. There are a few hours until Heath finishes work, and I'm still not sold on the hair dye decision.

I head for the hardware store to place an order for the things I'll need to start woodworking again, but on my way inside, I catch a glimpse of my reflection in the window. I look ... old.

My heart squeezes at the thought.

My grays haven't taken over yet, and in the dark, they're not as visible as they are when the sun hits them ... but they're not my only problem. The lines on my forehead and around my eyes are settling in, and while I don't *feel* like I'm approaching middle age, I ... I am.

The family thing is over. My wife is gone, my son has grown up, and without the goals of getting married, having kids, supporting my family, what do I have left?

This is the part no one talks about. The time that no one prepares you for.

I still have a whole lot of life left, but no idea what to do with it all.

Sure, I act like I'm obsessed with having sex because I'm a horny motherfucker, but it's also something that gives me a goal, something to work toward. After that ...

Fuck.

Nope.

I'm happy and excited and things are playing out exactly the way they're supposed to.

Everything is great. *Great* ...

After finishing up in the hardware store and telling Victor that I'll pick everything up once it's in, I make my way slowly toward the pharmacy.

The amount of stock they have is confronting, to say the least, and I check that no one I know is around before approaching the intimidating shelves of skin care options. I find it hard to believe any of the bullshit these products are claiming. Reduce wrinkles, plump skin, eliminate bags ...

The more I read through what's available, the more self-conscious I become about ... everything.

My hands and fingers are rough—do I need cream to fix that? Are my teeth too stained? Should I buy the whitening gel? Or the toothpaste? Or the fancy light thing? Do I need to wax my chest? My stomach? My fucking *armpits*?

A lump is building deep in my throat as the familiar pressure washes over me again. I'm so lost.

Figuring I'll start easy with the dye, I move to that aisle instead, but it's no better. Exactly how many shades of brown *are* there?

Goddamn.

I'm about to walk out with nothing, when I remember my reflection back at the hardware store and decide that screw it, I'm all in.

I grab a random box of dye, then fill my basket with every different type of skin stuff, some hand cream, face wash, cologne, and about five packets of breath mints.

If all this isn't enough to get me laid, I should give up now.

When I reach my car, I hesitate over going inside Killer Brew to see Art. I'm still not convinced that what Heath said about my dick size was a joke or not, and knowing Art, he'd be okay with taking a look to let me know. It's not something I've ever thought about before. I'm ... normal? I think? Is that even a thing? It's been a long time since I've been in a locker room with someone to compare myself to.

The problem is, I can try to fix everything else, but if size is actually something people care about, there's not much I can do there.

Maybe I'm better off not knowing.

Jesus fucking Christ. Will this self-consciousness ever end?

Chapter Nine

HEATH

I'm still kicking myself over the double booking by the time I leave work. In the end, all I could do was contact the guest and let them know they can't check in until a day later. I've offered them a complimentary night's stay as well as wine on arrival and free breakfast and dinner the day after.

It's a hit to our bottom line but will hopefully prevent a terrible review, which could be more damaging in the long run. I try not to take the failure personally. It doesn't work.

I call Mom on the way home, and she sounds as amused and exasperated as she usually does when I talk to her about my job. She's always so happy. Comforting. But there's a heaviness to her tone now that never used to be there, and I wish I could take it away.

I can't split myself in two, though, and for today, my focus is on Griff.

And my decision to stay and help him proves to be the right one when I get to his place and find him in the bathroom, staring at the sink, with about twenty jars, tubs, and tubes scattered around him.

"I feel like there's a story here."

"Am I *old*?" His loud question echoes faintly off the tile.

"Are you asking because you're feeling old, or you've forgotten your age?"

"That's it. Hair dye time."

Griff goes to storm by me, but I grab his elbow and push him back against the counter. "What's going on with you?"

"Nothing."

"*Griff.*" I reach up and give his earlobe a tug. The tense expression on his face melts and is replaced by an uncertain smile.

"I don't feel ..."

I try to wait him out, but it doesn't seem like he wants to continue. "Feel ..."

He pulls a face. "I don't think I'm ... I'm not ..."

"Yes?"

"Sexy, okay? I'm not sexy, and I'm worried we're going to go out and you'll find someone and have to ditch them because you feel sorry for me sitting all by myself."

What the hell is he talking about? I'm a bit in shock as I try to process how someone with the panty-melting rating of a thousand could actually think that.

I flick his forehead.

"Ouch." He jolts away from me. "What the hell was that for?"

"Thought your brain might need a jump start."

He scowls and turns to check his forehead in the mirror.

I scoff. "It wasn't that hard, you big baby."

"Hey, you have a lot of force behind those fingers."

"You should see what else they can do." I hold up three and wink at him in the mirror.

He responds with a flat look. "Are you here to help me or point out how stupid I am?"

"It depends." I cross my arms and lean back against the wall. "Are you going to say anything else stupid?"

"That wasn't stupid. I was being serious."

"I know you were. That's what makes it even worse."

His face falls as he picks up a jar of ... something. "This isn't going to get rid of the bags under my eyes, is it?"

"Not a chance" is my chipper reply. "Besides the fact you don't have any, this stuff is total crap. You want to look good? Drink water and get a decent sleep."

He mutters something I don't catch.

"You what now?"

"I haven't slept good all week," he says in a rush.

"Oh." This isn't an area I'm all that familiar with. "Why?"

"I'm not used to sleeping alone."

"Want me to buy you a sex doll?" I'm only half-joking. I'd do it if he asked, but he'd have to settle for a cheap blow-up one.

"With any luck, I'll find someone to blow my load with tomorrow, and then I'll sleep like a baby."

"Didn't Felix sleep like shit until he was, what, four?"

Griff hums. "Yeah, good point. I'll sleep like the dead, then."

"Sounds more accurate."

He clears his throat, then turns around, holding out a box of hair dye. "Please?"

"You're really set on that, aren't you?"

"If I can't fix this"—he waves a hand in front of his face—"then I can at least dye my hair and look a little better."

I screw up my face as I take the box, not sold on this at all. "I want it on the record that I think this is a horrible idea."

"Yeah, yeah, I get it. You're scared I'm going to steal all the guys."

"Sure. That's why." I take the box and lead the way out to the front porch, where we've set up camping chairs until Griff makes some proper ones. "You should leave the men for me and focus on the women."

His footsteps falter behind me. "Aren't you taking me to a gay bar?"

"I can if you want me to, but I thought someplace big would be better for your first time."

He shakes his head and drops into one of the chairs, long, thick legs stretched out in front of him. "Nah, let's go where you normally do."

He has no idea what he's getting himself into. And when he turns those vibrant blue eyes up at me, face open and hopeful, it occurs to me just how gorgeous Griffin is. Sweet and fun are two things I've always known, then the other night, there was a random hint of sexiness, but right now, looking down at him ... he's not going to have any problem hooking up. At all.

The thing he will have a problem with is not falling for whoever he hooks up with.

I got lucky with Poppy. It was hard sharing him with her at first, but we got along. There's no guarantee that will happen with whoever comes next.

I break eye contact and skim the directions on the back of the box. It sounds easy enough.

"Want to take off your shirt before we get started?"

"Sure." He strips out of it and settles back into the chair again, but not before I get an eyeful of back muscles.

"You're checking me out again," he says.

"I told you you're not going to have a problem tomorrow night."

He makes a skeptical noise while I take off my shirt just in case, then pull on the gloves and get to it. I work in silence for a couple of minutes while I get the hang of everything.

"Do you remember the rules I gave you?" I ask.

"No names. No bringing anyone home," he says.

"Well done."

"Getting teen throwbacks here for needing rules again."

"Don't." I don't like when he doubts himself. "You know your weaknesses, and you're working with them. That's a good thing."

"Well, let's hope. Otherwise, this time next week, I could be in a relationship again."

We both laugh, but mine is forced. I'm going to have to keep a closer eye on him than I thought.

"No strings, Griff," I remind him. "Harmless fun. We're living the bachelor life together."

"I'm going to fuck all of this up, aren't I?"

"Not if you don't want to."

But even saying that, I'm not convinced. He has a big heart, and when it comes to people he loves, he's committed. Poppy, Felix, me. He's always done whatever will make us happy, and I *know* if he finds someone kind and easy to talk to tomorrow night, he *will* ask for a name and number.

There's a chance they won't give it, of course.

But they'd be an idiot if they didn't.

When I think I have most of his hair covered, I massage it in, rubbing my fingers into his scalp. His head relaxes back into my grip as a rumbly moan catches in his throat, and while I know it's only because of the massage, that sound piques my interest. It's low and raw, and fucked if my cock gets the memo on who it is that made the sound.

"Harder ... yeah," he mutters. "That feels so good."

I have to close my eyes for a moment.

The massage—he means the massage, obviously.

But even as I remind myself of that fact, I'm picturing Griff naked in his kitchen again, cock in hand, murmuring about how good it feels.

Sweet Jesus, where are these thoughts coming from?

"Why are you breathing like that?" he asks, snapping me out of my thoughts.

"Like what?"

"All ... heavy ..."

Ah, shit, he's right. I could lie, but he knows me too well for that. "Because you have a filthy fucking mouth, Griff."

"What?"

I pitch my voice. "Oh, baby, that feels so good. Rub me harder, Heath. Get in there."

His answering laugh is loud. "What?"

"Your filthy talk and moaning like a porn star. Geez, man, I'm only human."

"You're turned on?"

I shift around to the front of him, continuing to massage in the dye. "What do you think?"

His attention drops to my shorts, where I'm sure the hard outline of my cock is visible. I'm so focused on his hair and not watching his face in an attempt to read his thoughts that I don't notice when he reaches up.

He skims over my V with the back of his finger, and a spear of arousal shoots down deep in my gut. My abs tense, and I suck in a breath, caught off guard at how good that felt.

"Sorry." His voice is husky. "Your skin looked ... warm."

"Warm?"

He swallows. "It's been a *really* long time."

Our eyes lock as my hands pause, and I read the uncertainty in his face as easily as my own thoughts.

What if we crossed that line ... just once?

It would be easy. He's hot, he's available, and I know him better than anyone in the world. If there was ever a man I could read perfectly in bed, could drive out of his mind with want, it'd be Griff.

It would be a disaster.

We both come to the conclusion at the exact same time. I hurry to pull back from him, and Griff jumps to his feet.

"All done?" he asks.

I nod, determined to pretend like whatever just happened was nothing. "I think so. It says we have to leave it for a bit, then you wash it out."

"Awesome. I thought that once it was done, we could go out tonight instead?"

Tonight? After this thing that happened-but-didn't-really, I'm not exactly eager to go out so soon.

"I'm not dressed for a night out." It's a total grasp at straws.

"We can duck by your place."

Of course we can, because that's the obvious solution.

Griff grabs us both a beer, and we sit outside, watching the sun set over the trees while we wait for enough time to pass before he can jump in the shower.

"Looks a bit dark." He's checking his reflection in his phone.

"It's wet. Wait until it's washed out and dry." I still think it's a bad idea, but he's done it now, so I'm going to be supportive.

A few minutes later, he disappears inside, and I hear the shower come alive. He takes his sweet-ass time, and I wonder if he's jerking off again. I kinda wish I had time to see to my own issue, because when he comes back, he's only wearing a towel. I drag my gaze away from him, staring out over his courtyard in an attempt to dissuade any inappropriate thoughts, but apparently, my traitorous brain has other ideas.

If I got on my knees and flicked open his towel, would he stop me?

Those kinds of questions are good for no one.

He asks about the bar in Springfield I'm planning to take him to, and I fill him in on it. There are usually a good mix of guys there. Most of them younger, but still a fair few around our age and older. He'll fit right in.

"So I think if you—" I cut off as I look at him again. "Ah, Griff? What color dye did you say you got again?"

"Brown, why?"

I open the camera on my phone and turn it toward him. "Because your hair is fucking black."

Chapter Ten

GRIFF

"I'd like to remind you that I said this was a horrible idea," Heath says as I stare into the mirror in dismay.

My hair is fucking black.

And some of the grays are *still* showing through.

I let out a long groan, and my asshole of a best friend laughs. He freaking *laughs*.

"What part of this is funny?"

"If you don't laugh, you'll cry, right?"

"Or I could kick your ass for doing this to me."

"Please," he breathes. "I was coerced."

Behind me, Heath picks up the box and flips it around to the front. I watch him in the mirror as he squints and tilts his head. "I suppose it sort of looks brown if I do this."

I appreciate him trying to make me feel better for my fuckup, but the truth is, I grabbed a box in the general vicinity of all the browns without paying attention. There were too many shades that I didn't think it would make a difference. I'm regretting that now.

"We could try to wash it—oh. Never mind, it's permanent."

"Oh no."

"You don't look too bad ..."

I grunt and turn away from the depressing sight. "I look ridiculous."

He bites his lip, and I know he's trying to hold in agreeing with me.

You can't fool me, I tell him.

I'm trying really hard though, his expression says right back.

"I'm going to order pizza since I'm not going anywhere like this."

"Extra—"

"Pepperoni." Like I didn't already know that.

"So, night in," Heath says as we return to sitting on the porch.

The sun has almost disappeared, leaving behind the scent of flowers and constant buzz of whatever insects are lurking.

"This doesn't help my problem," I point out.

"It's only hair. Chances are in a club, people won't even notice."

"It's not about the other people," I explain. "I wanted to *feel* like I looked good. For confidence."

His mouth forms an O. "So you can talk to people."

"Exactly."

Heath slaps my thigh. Hard. "You're not *supposed* to be talking to people, dumbass. I can only speak for other men here, but we don't need limericks to suck your dick. You go up to a dude on the dance floor, grind a little, nod to the restrooms, and get it over and done with."

"You make it sound so easy."

"That's because there's nothing to it. Get their age and their consent, then get busy."

My lips purse briefly. "I don't need to be asking for ages."

"Trust me, you do. There are some pretty twinks out there, so you want to be sure."

I chuckle. "I bet. But I don't need ages because I'm not interested in anyone who looks like they could be Felix's age. Whether they are or not."

"So what are you looking for?"

I rub my jaw as I think. It's not like I have a checklist to work off; attraction for me isn't something that follows a set list of criteria. And it's less physical to me, and more ... a vibe? An aura? "No clue."

"You're telling me you haven't spent the last few months imagining this scenario?"

"Of course I have, but whenever I picture myself with someone, they're faceless with no detail." Except for when I think of Heath.

"Blond or brunet?"

"Either. Both."

"This is going to be easy for you, then." He sniggers. "Who do you find attractive? Like, who was the last person you saw and were like *yep, they're hot*?"

"You."

His head snaps in my direction, making me laugh.

"You can't be surprised—it happened maybe half an hour ago." I've already broken my first rule when it comes to him.

"I thought that was more of a proximity thing."

"Probably is. Proximity and circumstance. It's not like I've ever looked at you like that before."

"Never?"

I glance over to find Heath's eyes narrowed playfully. "Okay, fine. Yes. I've noticed you're good-looking, but not in an I-want-to-jump-you type of way. More that if I looked like you, I'd never have to worry." My gaze strays to him again, and I can tell the difference between looking at him now to the times I've admired him before. He's gorgeous. Winning smile, kind eyes, long legs, and lean muscles. He's polished to perfection. But does that mean I could ever actually go there? Who knows? "What about you?" I find myself asking. "You ever looked at me like that?"

"Total honesty?"

"Of course."

"Nope. I had a crush for a minute in high school, but my taste in men is very different to you."

Huh. That's ... a good thing. Isn't it? So why does his answer piss me off? "Then ... the other night, and today ..."

He hesitates before shrugging and having another sip of his beer. "Apparently, seeing you haul lumber is a weakness of mine."

I don't mean it to happen, but I can't push down the smug feeling. "So rough and tough is how you like it?"

"Nope. Normally I like to be the one in charge."

"You? Control issues? I never would have guessed," I say dryly.

"Hey, you're the one attracted to a total boss, so what does that say about you?"

My cheeks heat even as I say, "Good taste?"

"Damn straight it is." Heath holds up his hand for a high five, and I switch my beer to the other hand to meet it.

I know I shouldn't push my luck, but the words come out anyway. "Geez ... Imagine us hooking up? What a disaster."

"You clearly don't know how good I am in bed."

It's my turn for my head to snap around. Heath is grinning, stirring me up, and while the part of me that's known him for years is cringing away at the conversation, the part that's been wanting to get laid for way too long won't let me.

"Well, of course you'd say that about yourself."

"You saying I'm full of shit?"

I tilt my beer his way. "Just saying it's easy enough to claim that when you know I'd never find out if you were lying."

"If you think I won't put my money where my mouth is,

I'm getting the impression you don't know me well at all, Griffy-boy."

"You're saying you'd suck my dick, then?"

"Sure."

And that's the second time he's surprised me in one conversation because I never expected him to admit it. "No way."

"Way."

"I thought you said it didn't measure up."

He laughs. "Two things. First, again, not speaking for women, but other than a few size queens, no one gives a fuck about your size. Just how you use it. Second, you have *nothing* to worry about in that department."

"Well, thank you for making me so stressed about it all day that I dyed my hair black."

"Did ... did you think that would make it grow? I don't know if you need to hear this, but that shit isn't fertilizer."

"Why the hell do I put up with you?"

"My loveable nature."

Damn him, it's true. "You *are* pretty loveable."

"Cheers, man. You too."

"But, ah, we seriously need to cool it on the teasing," I say. "My cock can't take much more of it."

"Is this more rules for you?"

"I suppose it is. You want me to keep things platonic, and let's face it, if something happened between us, there's no way I'd be able to draw that line."

Heath chuckles. "You saying you'd get attached to me?"

"Considering I haven't been able to shake you for over

twenty-five years, I'm saying I already am." I glance over to find Heath watching me, a strange look on his face.

But then we trade matching smiles, and as much as we tease and fake flirt, and despite the occasional boner, I know nothing is going to change this. This smart, fun—and apparently *sexy*—man is with me until the end.

Chapter Eleven

HEATH

I can't convince Griff to go out over the weekend, not that I try very hard. I should. He needs it. But when he says he wants to stay in on Saturday night, I agree.

I tell myself it's because his hair looks ridiculous, and it does—there are dye stains around his hairline and ears, plus it washes him out—but I don't think that's where the relief comes from.

"Hey," Griff mutters, walking into the reception Monday morning. It's bright in here with the morning sun pouring through the high skylights. He has a cap pulled down over his hair, but there's no missing how much darker it is. It almost looks like a wig. He's also back in a flannel shirt, which I'm going to have to train him out of if he plans on spending more time in the office.

My gaze trails down his broad back as he passes me, and surprisingly, I find myself warming to the material. You know you've reached desperation when even flannel looks good.

"Don't you own any business wear?" I ask him.

There isn't a dress policy here, but it goes without saying that we need to be professional, which is why I've always worn suits. Nothing stuffy—I try to match the place with bright colors and patterns, pants tailored to hug my ankles, and no ties—but it's a good deal more professional than Griff ever looks.

"You know I don't." Something in his voice catches my attention.

"You okay?"

"Fine. Just worried."

"About?"

He joins me behind the reception desk, large body warmed from the sun and heating the space between us. "Poppy's back today. Wants to start showing me some things."

"So she's definitely leaving, then?"

"Yup. Called a meeting for later in the week to let everyone know."

We're quiet, and I try to hold back from watching him out of the corner of my eye. "You going to miss her?"

"No—well, yes, obviously—but it's not that."

"You're worried about the work stuff?"

He scowls and rubs a hand over his face. "Exactly."

"You're a smart guy, Griff. You'll get it."

His mouth forms a line before the frustration bleeds from his face. A large, warm hand comes to rest on my lower back. "You'll stay with us today, won't you? I mean, you already know everything, but in case there's something she's missed showing you, I want to know you at least have things covered."

This is going to be fun. Knowing more about what to do around here than the person running the place. It's lucky it's him, because anyone else and I would have told them to go to hell already. "Of course. Like I keep saying, you're not alone in this."

At least for as long as I'm here, anyway.

Griff breathes a soft laugh, shoulders releasing his tension. His cheeks go pink behind his scruff, and then he reaches up and awkwardly tugs my ear before hurrying away. I watch the office door as he closes it, feeling ... something. Something making my chest feel a bit bigger.

I go back to checking the reservations and push it from my mind.

The news of Poppy leaving goes down the way I thought it would. Shock and disappointment over losing her, a few worried looks thrown Griff's way.

I know everything going through their minds, and as

much as I love Griff, they're right to worry. We enjoy working here, and they pay us well; none of us wants the resort being left in the hands of someone who will only run it into the ground.

Instead of my concerns easing over the week, they only get worse, because with every day that passes, I become more and more worried that Griff isn't going to get it. He's smart and he's genuinely trying, but he doesn't *get* computers. He has a smartphone, but that's as far as he's gotten when it comes to technology, and most of the time, he only uses it to make phone calls.

He's never had a reason to use a computer.

By Friday, Poppy and Griff are at each other's throats. I want to remind her it's partially her fault for never letting him do anything, but he's a big boy. If he wanted to learn all of this, there was nothing stopping him.

"I need a break." He pushes away from the desk and walks out of the office.

Poppy takes off her glasses and rubs her eyes. "What else can I do?" she says.

"He just needs time."

She aims a bemused smile my way. "Loyal to a fault. As always. But even you can tell this isn't going well."

Well, obviously, I'm not blind. She's going over everything too quickly, and he's not asking her to slow down either. I'm beginning to understand the communication issues they had in their marriage.

"We're throwing a lot at him," I remind her.

"I suppose. But don't you ..."

"What?"

She sighs. "Do you think he's also not trying either? Like maybe if he keeps saying he can't do it, it'll make me stay?"

I frown and remind myself to think through my response before snapping at her in his defense. Poppy might be the ex-wife, but she's not some kind of evil caricature. "Do you mean *here* or *together*?"

"Here, obviously. Neither of us wants the relationship to last a minute longer than it needs to. But running this place is a lot of work, and you know how Griffin is content to do the least amount possible."

Well, that's blatantly incorrect. Maybe he doesn't do any of the office work, but he's taken on a huge task here by himself. It's not easy work to maintain the grounds and gardens, to keep up on repairs and updates. He buoys the staff through his happy energy, and he's always the first to talk to people about the flowers he's planted or what there is to do in town. He doesn't do the books, but he's the heart and soul of this place.

Again, the urge to tell her off for speaking about him like that is strong, but ... well, I understand why she thinks that way. Griff likes to keep things simple. "Actually, he's very hardworking, but whatever he's working on has to hold his interest. Numbers on a spreadsheet, accounting software, and bookings and reservations doesn't do that."

Not like his woodwork does. He's already crafted the beginning of two chairs out of the lumber we ... collected? —*stole*?—with no signs of slowing down.

"There's no way I could leave without you here," she says. "Thank you so much for stepping up."

"It's Griff," I remind her. "Like I'd ever say no to him."

"You're both very close," she says, gaze dropping back to the desk. "But you're allowed to say no when you need to. You're allowed to put yourself first every now and then."

I've put myself first for most of my life. I went out when I wanted, I hooked up when I wanted. I bought the apartment I wanted and eat when and what I like. "You don't need to worry. I'm always my first priority."

"Uh-huh. Which is how you ended up working here."

"What do you mean?"

"Well, it was a small little hole-in-the-wall when we first got started. It took a lot to get it off the ground, and you knew we needed the help, so you jumped right in. It's the same with Griff now. He needs you, you're there."

"And I always will be."

She gives me a grateful smile. "I'm so glad he has you in his corner, but my reminder stands. Griff is important, but so are you. If that means making him get off his ass to do something for you in return, then do it."

"Noted."

Not that I need her help when it comes to him. Our friendship has outlasted their relationship, and even though I know she cares about us both, I'm also not a fan of her acting like she knows Griff better than I do.

They might have been the ones having sex, but I'm the one he's always talked to. The one he's always shared everything with.

I know more about his stresses and worries and what makes him happy than she ever has.

And I'm not sure where this hostility toward Poppy is coming from since I love her. She's family. She, Griff, and Felix are mine, and even though things are changing between them, it doesn't change my relationship with the three of them.

Only, this need to defend Griff against her is new.

The rational side of me knows she isn't being mean, that she cares about him, but ... the irrational side simply doesn't give a fuck.

I've never let anyone speak negatively about him, and I'm not about to start now.

The best way to change the way she views him is to get him back on track. To help him run this place like the confident, capable guy he is and help him shake the funk he's fallen into.

And even though I get this nasty knot in my gut, I know it all starts with hooking up with someone. He's stressed about making that step, and it's bleeding through to other areas of his life.

"Also, I didn't want to ask," Poppy says. "But what did he do to his hair?"

That makes me laugh, and the momentary hostility I felt toward her dissolves. "It's a long story."

"Well, I don't need to hear it, but do everyone a favor and get him to a salon to fix that ASAP."

A salon? "But it's permanent."

"They can fix it; they're professionals. Who—if he

wanted to color his hair—he should have gone to in the first place."

I add making an appointment to my mental list and then go in search of him. There's still a long afternoon ahead of us.

DMC Group Chat

Griff: *Heath's dragging me to Springfield to buy clothes.*

Orson: *What for?*

Griff: *Going out. To clubs. I dunno, it feels so WEIRD to me*

Art: *Clubs are the best. You drink, you dance, you sweat, you get your dick sucked ...*

Orson: *Leaving Art to his reminiscing, why Springfield? We have clothing stores here.*

Griff: *That's what I asked. He laughed at me but I never got an answer!*

Art: *Hahahah please.*

Griff: *See? Just like that!*

Orson: *Maybe it's gay guy speak?*

Payne: *Translation: the clothes here aren't hot enough.*

Orson: *There you go.*

Art: *I'm coming, by the way.*

Payne: *I hope he's talking about actually going somewhere and not what he's currently doing.*

Art: *What? You don't jerk off while messaging your homies?*

Payne: ...

Orson: ...

Griff: *I know I'm inexperienced, but there's no way people do that.*

Art: ...

Payne: *He HAS to be fucking with us.*

Art: *Let's all just pretend I'm talking about Griff putting on a fashion show. You will be putting on a fashion show for us, right?*

Orson: *Oh, I want in on that! When are we going?*

Griff: *No way*

Art: *What? We can't miss this. It will be your debut. The moment your butterfly emerges.*

Orson: *You realize you have to agree or he's going to keep at that, right?*

Payne: *So we're all just ignoring Art's jerking off then?*

Orson: *I think it's for the best.*

Payne: *Sorry I can't make it, Griff. I'll be busy scrubbing that image from my mind.*

Griff: *No one will make it, there's no fashion show. You'll never let me live down the hair.*

Orson: ... *hair?*

Art: *Oh, this is gonna be good.*

Chapter Twelve

GRIFF

"Is this really necessary?" I ask as Heath drags me into the store. Apparently the clothing choices in Kilborough aren't good enough, so Heath has hauled my ass all the way to Springfield to buy things for work and going out.

"For the thousandth time, yes," he says. "Now quit your whining. We're making a day of it. Relax."

"Relax," he says, like that's so easy to do. I know nothing about clothes, least of all ones that are appropriate to wear to an office, and the pressure of getting dressed up every day doesn't fit in with my idea of a relaxed life.

Besides, my denim jacket is feeling really out of place here. Heath of course looks incredible, damn him. All golden skin and brown hair and bright, sparkly teeth. I wonder if he whitens them. Should I whiten mine? I run a hand self-consciously over the hat I'm wearing. Considering the clusterfuck of my last self-improvement, maybe I'll table the teeth whitening for now.

A cheer goes up as we walk into the fancy-ass place, and my gut drops through the floor when I find Art and Orson waiting for us.

What in the ever-loving divorced-juice-drinking shit is this?

"Thought you'd never show up," Art says.

I cringe out a smile. "I wouldn't have if I knew you were here. *How* are you here? I never gave details."

The dark look I throw Heath's way only makes him laugh. He slaps me on the ass—and *hello*, inappropriate reaction in my pants—before passing me and dropping down into the space next to Orson.

I wave a finger in their direction. "And what's all this?"

"Emotional support panel," Orson says. "Who will not be mentioning the hair."

"Plus, we wanted a perv," Art adds, *so* helpfully.

My cheeks heat as I plant my hands on my hips. "In other words, you're here to make this as uncomfortable as possible for me."

"Bingo." Art pumps his eyebrows.

I try not to grimace.

"Come on, Griff. No sulking. The flannel will be there for you when you get home." Heath jumps up and plants his hands on my shoulders to steer me away from the dressing rooms to the racks of clothes. "We're going to find you some sexy power suits, and then we can play employer/employee where you call me into your office for disciplinary action."

I choke on my spit. "You have an overactive imagination."

"And you have an ass that's going to look sexy as fuck in these pants." Heath passes over some navy dress pants before ducking down the aisles of clothes and piling my arms high with options. When a salesperson comes over to ask if we need help, Heath waves him away, despite the "help me" eyes I'm making.

So much for being in and out.

I let out a loud exhale that catches Heath's attention, and he turns his warm brown eyes on me.

"Say it after me: relaxxx."

"Fuck offff."

He throws his head back with a laugh. "It's cute you think that will deter me when I'm dying to get you into one of these tight shirts."

My face falls, and he must get that I'm not playing because he steps close and lowers his voice.

"We're all here because we love you. Art and I might give you shit, but Orson's right. We're here for support and to give you confidence." He nudges me. "You could do with a healthy heaping of that."

"Me? Unconfident? Now, what gives you that idea?"

He reaches under the hat and gently tugs my hair. "Hmm, yeah, no idea."

I'm sorely tempted to bury my face in the pile of clothes.

Then Heath pulls out a pair of tiny shorts. "And these are for the weekend." He slaps my ass again, and *again*, my cock reacts.

"Why do you keep doing that?" I ask.

"Copping a feel. Duh."

"Jesus, we both need to get laid."

"Yup. That's exactly it."

I grab the shorts and go to put them back on the shelf when Heath closes his arms around me and awkwardly half marches and half drags me back toward the change rooms.

"Let me have my fun," he begs.

"No fucking way."

"The shorts are so sexy though."

"I don't care how sexy they are, I'm not trying them on."

His pitying moan is so close to my ear, it sends shivers through me. "Please, Griff. It's been so long I need something sexy to look at."

The gravelly note to his voice is making my goddamn body react *again*. He's not playing fair. And ... I'm not sure I want him to.

Rule number ten for keeping things platonic: *don't* try on shorts that will turn your best friend on.

And rule number eleven: don't fucking want to.

But even when we get back to the change rooms and I'm faced with the mountain of things I need to get through, my hand gravitates toward the shorts.

I'm being an idiot. I'm dangerously close to that line.

But it's been a long time since anyone showed me interest—fake or not. And maybe I *do* want to feel like I can be as hot as Heath thinks. Even if it's total bullshit and only for a second.

Chapter Thirteen

HEATH

Griff radiates awkwardness as he walks into the changing rooms, but these little nudges outside of his comfort zone are what he needs to take this next step.

A next step that I *know* is necessary, and as much as I want to help him with it, I need to sit out for this one. Fuck, it's hard though.

I want to slap myself, because what the hell? Griff is my number one. I want to be there for him through everything and to support him with whatever he needs support for. It's how we've always been. And I knew with the split coming up that the first step would be to take him out and get his dick wet—hell, I was looking forward to it—and now ... I'm hesitating. It's completely unlike me.

"What do you think of Ford?" Orson asks while we wait.

The mechanic?

I glance over at him, but he's looking around the store, and I can't tell if he's actually *looking* or if he's distracting himself. "He's cool," I say. I've been out in Springfield with him a couple of times. "Why?"

"Eh, no reason."

"There is definitely a reason." Art spins to fully face Orson. "Out with it."

Orson gives Art a soft smile. "I know you think you smell gossip, but there's none here. Ford asked me out, I told him I was straight, that's it."

"Then why did you want to know about him?" I ask, smelling bullshit.

"I've never been asked out by a man before. It was different."

Art starts laughing. "And you didn't say no."

"What?"

"You said he asked you out and you told him you were straight." Art shrugs. "That's not a no."

"Of course it is."

"I hate to say it, but I'm with Orson on this one." What's Art getting at?

"As someone who has asked out many men over the years, there is a big difference between a *no* or a *sorry I'm not interested* and an *I'm straight*."

"There is?" Orson sounds torn between confused and interested.

"A big difference. The ones who throw out their straightness like armor are usually the ones I'm sucking off by the end of the night."

Orson's mouth drops. "They tell you they're straight and you hit on them anyway?"

"Nope. I'm good at reading people. If they toss out a *No, sorry, I'm straight*, then I let them go. But if there's no *no*, I let them know to find me if they change their mind."

Orson looks like he's lost the will to speak.

I chuckle. "I'm surprised you haven't been punched in the face yet."

"Bold of you to assume I haven't."

A throat clears, and I look up as the change room door cracks open and Griff pokes his head out. "Don't say shit."

"Shit," Art and I say at the same time.

Orson punches my shoulder. "Supportive."

"That." Griff points at him. "Support, please. One dickish comment and I'm out of here."

Art agrees, and as subtly as I can, I tug on my earlobe and give Griff a wink. The tension melts from his face, and the door swings open.

I fucking swallow my fucking tongue.

He's wearing a deep-V T-shirt and the shorts I grabbed for him thinking there's no way in hell he'd put them on, but there they are in all their thigh-hugging, cock-cupping glory. I can't look away. My mouth feels abnormally dry, and I try to remind myself this is my best friend, this is *Griffin*, and sure I flirt with him, but I don't actually *mean* it.

But looking at him … I think I might actually mean it.

The shorts are cuffed, barely reach his hairy, muscular thighs, and the imprint of his cock rivals the way his full ass is trying to burst through the seams.

"I look ridiculous," he says, face blazing red.

Art scoffs. "Ridiculous isn't the word you're looking for, if the way my cock has perked up in support is any indication."

"Jesus ..." Griff mutters.

"I'm with Art." Orson shifts. "I think we're all a bit gay right now."

"*And* I'm getting changed aga—"

"Wait."

Griff pauses at the word, eyes flying to lock with mine. The poor guy looks like a deer caught in the headlights, but even as I break his stare and let my gaze drop, he doesn't move.

My eyes trail over his chest, his thick torso, all the way back to those shorts. My tongue grazes my dry lips, and I know I need to look away, but damn, I want to push Griff into that change room and drop to my knees, fuck who's around to witness it.

These aren't thoughts I should be having around him.

I can't get control of them though.

All I can do is hope that once we go out and the both of us get some action, this sexual tension will disappear again.

"You're buying those," I say, my voice a hoarse croak. "*I'm* buying those. For this weekend. Your outfit is my treat."

"Heath ..."

I shake my head and meet his eyes again. "Get them."

He swallows and then finally nods. "Okay."

Chapter Fourteen

GRIFF

The whole time I'm having my hair done, I feel like an idiot. The stylist had a giggle at my home job before steering me to a chair to get started. She's pretty and chatty, with no ring on her finger, and I consider asking for her number when she's done, but a second later, I dismiss the idea.

She's borderline too young-looking for my taste. Plus, I know her name. And where she works, which is definitely against the rules Heath set out for me.

Since I'm determined to prove Heath and his theory about me always getting attached wrong, when I walk out of there, I don't regret my decision.

If I wasn't planning to go out tonight, I might not have been so strong.

Heath lives just off the main street in a one-bedroom

apartment. Unlike my place, his "minimal" decorating is on purpose, and he's created the ideal bachelor pad. If I didn't know him and he brought me back here, you could guarantee he'd be getting laid. It's as confident and polished as he is. Long, low, leather couch, a huge flat-screen, and even a floor rug, which I never in a million years would have thought to buy for my own place.

I've always loved his apartment more than my own house.

He answers the door with a huge smile and a towel around his waist, hair still dripping from his shower.

My focus immediately drops to the one lone water droplet sliding over his abs, and my mouth goes dry.

"Are you trying to torture me?" I get out.

He snorts and steps aside. "Hey to you, too."

"The last few times we've hung out, I've been close to jumping you, and now you answer the door like that. It's almost like you want it to happen."

Heath's warm, deep laugh doesn't help the situation. "Calm down, cowboy. I had to drop by work this morning to settle something with a supplier, and then by the time I got back from picking up food, I was running late."

"Likely story." I'm teasing—mostly. Sure, Heath is hot. And I thought about him while I jerked off in the kitchen last week, and the shower ... multiple times ... but crossing lines there would be too strange. Not only does it risk our friendship, but do I really want to see my best friend's orgasm face?

Hard no.

I don't think.

I need to get this horniness out of my system.

As I pass the kitchen, I toss my phone and wallet down on the dark stone counter and glance over at where Heath is watching me. "What?"

"Your hair ..."

I run my hand self-consciously over it. "Is it better?"

"It looks good. You might have a chance of getting laid now, after all."

"Your confidence in me is overwhelming." I cross to get some water. "I almost asked for the hair stylist's number."

Heath groans. "You didn't."

"I didn't because I remembered your rules." And it didn't seem right. "I felt like I was supposed to." It's not until I say it does it occur to me that's the case.

"We've been over this. You don't have to do anything you don't want to."

"Yeah, I know. So where are these clothes?" Changing the subject works, and Heath stops looking at me too hard. He's always been good at reading me, and for some reason, I'm paranoid about what it is he might see.

"Let me get dressed, and I'll bring them out."

He leaves to pad down the short hall toward his bedroom, and I lean around the corner, admiring the way the light blue towel molds perfectly over his ass.

I pull my eyes away. This isn't good.

Making him a point of attraction because he's the first available person since my split isn't smart. I need him. For more than sex. If I screwed everything up between us, it'd feel like losing ... everything.

Walking away from Poppy was doable. We had an expiry date, and things were mutual. But the thought of losing Heath creates this ache in my chest I don't think I'd ever recover from.

I need to stick to my rules.

Number ... I dunno, fifty? Stop looking at his ass.

I manage to get myself to relax again, which lasts until he calls me into his room and hands my clothes over.

And even though I tried them on earlier in the week, I don't remember them being this tight. Then again, I don't remember much from that shopping trip but the way Heath looked at me.

"What the ..." I pluck at the button-up T-shirt I'm wearing, seriously worried the buttons are about to burst off and hit the mirror. The shorts are no better. They're just as tight, and there isn't nearly enough material.

"Hot."

I catch Heath's eyes in the mirror. "They look like they don't fit."

"No, they look like they're supposed to be taken off. Which is definitely the effect you want." He grabs my shoulder and turns me to the side. "Look at your ass." Then, to drive the point home, he runs his hand over it and gives it a squeeze. Lust makes my balls ache, but I shake it off.

Rule number *eight-fucking-hundred*: no asking Heath to touch me again.

I turn back to the front, but he doesn't step back. I'm so

aware of him behind me that rule eight hundred is hard to follow. "No one will be looking at my ass when these shorts have my cock on full display." The familiar panic of being out of my depth creeps in, and I have to move away from the mirror before I chicken out of going. Just like last weekend. I'm almost grateful for the shitty dye job because it bought me more time.

I drop onto the side of Heath's bed and force myself to breathe.

"What's going on?" he asks.

"I feel stupid," I answer honestly. "Aren't I too old to be wearing things like this? I'm worried people will think I'm trying too hard."

He waves a hand over himself as he sits beside me. "We're the same age, man, and I've never had a complaint."

"Yeah, but you're *you*. You don't look old. You don't have a fully grown kid. You're not divorced and starting over. Your incredible body is made for clothes like these."

Heath's fingers find my chin, and he turns my head to look at him. "Is that what this is about?" he asks softly. "What happened to all that stuff Art is always saying about divorce being a fresh start? Because I know I give him hell for it, but he's right."

"Easy to say, harder to believe."

"The only way to believe it is to put it into practice."

He's right. I just never thought it'd be so difficult. Turns out being separated is a whole lot harder than I thought it would be. This illusion of the simple life that I had for my future is disappearing quickly, and I'm clinging to Heath like my life raft.

"We're going out," I say. "And I'm wearing this."

"You sure?"

"Nope."

He leans in until his breath dances over my neck. "Would you be more sure if I told you how sexy you are? And that I can guarantee you're going to be getting off with someone in only a few hours."

I draw a shaky inhale. "You can't know that."

"I do though." He leans in farther. "Because if you don't find someone while we're out, I'll drag you back here and do the job myself."

My head snaps toward him so fast our noses bump. "What did we say about teasing?"

His brown eyes are locked on my lips, faint line dimpling the middle of his forehead. Then he pulls back suddenly, and it's like he takes all the warmth in the room with him. "No teasing, that's how confident I am. I can say it all I like because I know there's no way I'll have to follow through."

Of course. No way. He's trying to make me feel good. To give me confidence.

Instead, all his words manage to do is make me second-guess more than ever.

Chapter Fifteen

HEATH

I take Griff to a gay bar in Springfield that I frequent often. It's casual downstairs with karaoke and drag queen shows, but upstairs is where they have the dance floor and—on Saturday nights—men in thongs dancing in cages.

Let's say no one comes here for their top-shelf liquor.

The good thing about this gay bar is that by the time midnight rolls around, you've got a room full of horny men, and someone like Griff will have his pick of the bunch. With how anxious he is, I've gotta skew the odds in his favor.

Especially if I don't want to have to follow through on what I said to him before I left.

Which I don't. Because I was teasing him. Obviously.

And now I'm clearly trying to convince myself of that rather than stating a fact.

I'm sitting at the bar, back firmly turned to the dance floor, but it doesn't stop me from catching glimpses of Griff in the mirror every now and then.

When we first got here, he was way too anxious to dance, and it took me pulling him out there and loosening him up to stop him shredding the label on his beer bottle. As soon as the first guy made eyes at him, I pushed them together and slipped away.

I lift my drink and glare at the glass. I have no idea what's in this, but since I started drinking it, my mood has taken a nosedive.

There's none of that lovely buzz. Just a rotten feeling in my gut and aggressive buzzing in my fingertips. I push it away, then give in to the urge to turn around and watch.

Griff is dancing between two guys who look ready to maul him at any second. My gaze tracks one beefy arm down to where the man's hand is resting on Griff's hip, and my nausea increases.

I remind myself this is good; this is exactly what Griff needs. He's being shown attention—a fucking *lot* of it—and it'll be helping his confidence at the same time. It's getting full in here, approaching the time of night where people will slink away for quickies, and while I've encouraged Griff this whole time, it's not something I need to see.

If I didn't feel so not myself tonight, I'd be out there finding someone of my own to sneak away with. There's still plenty of time. Surely Griff isn't ready to take on two guys at once, so maybe I could slide up to the wiry guy behind Griff and take him off Griff's hands.

But to do that, I'd have to drag my focus away from where that man is touching *my* best friend.

A spike of annoyance hits me right in the chest, and I glance up to find Griff watching me.

Am I actually doing this? his slightly panicked stare asks me.

And no matter how I might be feeling, I send him a reassuring smile before turning back to the bar, ignoring the way my heart squeezes.

With any luck, Griff will disappear with one of those guys soon, and then we can get out of here. I'm in no mood to hook up. One of the barmen has already taken my glass, and since I'm not going to be doing anything else for the next hour, I figure I should order another.

Maybe the answer to this grossness inside me isn't to stop drinking but to get so drunk it numbs the feeling altogether.

Just as I lift my hand to get someone's attention, a thick arm wraps around my waist. I'm about to tell whoever it is to fuck off when lips press to my ear, and a familiar voice growls, "Come dance with me."

My gaze finds Griff in the bar mirror, hot and sweaty and pressed against me. I was right that it wouldn't take long for his shirt to disappear.

I lean into him. "What happened to those guys you were dancing with?"

"Dunno." His arm tightens. "Don't care."

A shiver races through me when I turn and our eyes

clash. Even in the dark, his are so goddamn blue I find it hard to look away.

Without a word, I slide from my stool and let him lead the way. The room is humid, bodies crushed together, music thumping, the smell of fresh sweat filling my senses, but none of it means anything when Griff's hands find the bottom of my shirt.

Hot? his eyes ask.

I help him push my shirt off, then tuck it into the back of my shorts like he's done to his.

Griff's hands find my waist, almost nervously and at complete odds with how confident he was getting me out here. I rest my hands on his arms, give him time, let him relax, not sure what's happening here but ready to go with it anyway.

We dance with a good amount of distance between us, every inch feeling like a solid wall I need to push through. But slowly, bit by bit, the space disappears until I'm pressed against him. His hands slide around to my back while I bury one hand into his hair and let the other drop to his hip.

I grip him in the exact way that man did earlier, and the rotten feeling in my gut loosens its hold.

Griff is mine. At least for right now. The sexy man with cautious smiles, who's lost and uncertain but still has that spark in him that draws me near.

I turn in his arms, and he pulls me flush against him. His coarse chest hair rubs against my back as he dips his head, running his nose along my neck to where it meets my shoulder.

My skin pebbles under his touch, and I can't tell if it's the heat in the room or the large warm body behind me, but my blood is running hot. I arch my neck to give him more access, and when Griff's tongue runs over it, a shudder races through me.

With my back to him, it should be easy enough to forget who it is touching me, but my brain seems desperate to cling to the knowledge that it's Griff.

His hand splays over my lower stomach and presses me back until my ass nestles against his groin, and I almost laugh.

He's hard.

Of course he's hard.

Griff doesn't have any other setting.

And the smart thing to do would be to put an end to this ... whatever now, but my ass doesn't get the message, because it presses harder against him. Griff's fingers flex, and I'm sure I make out a groan over the music. It's fucking perfect. Sexy.

Shit. I should have tried to find a hookup of my own, because now I'm here ... it's not a joke anymore.

I want him.

Desperately.

Griff's hand inches lower, fingers flirting with the hem of my shorts, and I know exactly what it is he wants.

We've reached the line. The very faint fucking line between a decades-long friendship and a move that could ruin us. This is the point I'm supposed to step away. The point where my guidance ends and Griff moves on without me.

I know what I'm supposed to do, but that doesn't stop me from lacing my fingers through his and guiding his hand down to my cock.

"Oh, *fuck*," he gasps into my ear.

I let go of his hand, but Griff doesn't release me. He squeezes tighter, grips harder, and then suddenly his hands are back on my hips, and he spins me in his arms.

Griff holds me tight as we dance, hips perfectly aligned, hard cocks pressing together while his hands squeeze bruises into my ass.

I'm not sure whether to look at him or if it will shatter the moment, but even with all reason going out of the window, the one thing that will always come first is making sure Griff is okay.

I glance down at him, checking in that he's comfortable with this or if he needs me to stop, but the heated glare he sends my way answers my question perfectly.

I dare you to try and end this.

I dig both hands into his hair this time. It's so soft, smells amazing, but even better than that is the scent of Griff's overheated skin. I bury my nose into his neck, breathing in the smell of his sweat and driving myself wild. My balls are aching for him, and the friction of his cock against mine is simmering at a level that could very quickly get out of control.

I need to kiss him, but I can't bring myself to close the distance. I'm acutely aware of who I'm holding and who I'm touching as I drag my lips over his jaw. My gut is knotted with desire, and even as my higher reasoning claims that kissing Griff would be awkward and uncomfortable, my lips won't quit. They skim the scruff on his cheek, moving closer and closer until they brush the corner of his mouth.

I tighten my hands in his hair, holding him close, then kiss that same spot again.

Griff's lips part, sucking in a sharp, sudden breath.

I'm about to take my first taste of his mouth when Griff cups my chin and pulls back.

"You promised I'd get off with someone tonight," he rasps.

"I did."

"What if I only want to get off with you?"

Chapter Sixteen

GRIFF

Rule number *seventeen thousand and twenty-four*: do not have sex with Heath.

Except the rule book is long forgotten as we get back to his apartment and he fumbles to unlock his door. I've never been this desperate for someone, and that's saying a lot since I'm always so horny. I might be inexperienced with hookups, but desperation is something I have plenty of past experience to draw from, and I have never, *ever*, been so fucking desperate.

Heath's door swings forward, and we stumble after it. I'm plastered to his back, not able to stop my hands from mapping out every inch of skin I can reach. Having another body against mine is indescribable, but knowing it's Heath takes that feeling and intensifies it.

Why shouldn't my first hookup be with my best friend?

It's almost a no-brainer that he should be the first man I ever have sex with.

I kick the door closed behind us, and Heath's fingers link with mine.

"Through here." His voice is husky and deep, giving me a good indication he's feeling as overwhelmed as I am.

I follow him to his room, a place I've been so many times before, but this time when we reach his bed, we know there's no turning back. I press close behind him as I strip him out of his shirt again and then reach around to pop the button on his shorts.

"Feeling confident?" he asks.

"Just trying not to think too hard."

"Excellent strategy." He turns in my arms before I can get him fully naked and helps me out of my shirt and shorts. "Goddamn ..."

I give my freed cock a stroke, loving the way he watches every movement. "Are you going to get on the bed, or will I have to make you?" I ask.

I'm rewarded with the flash of a smile before he drops back onto his mattress, and I climb up over the top of him. Heath is gorgeous. Lean muscle, round shoulders, and everything about him feels warm and inviting.

I reach up to run my thumb over his pale, soft lips. "You gonna kiss me?"

"Do you want me to?"

"No. Fuck, Heath, I need it."

He grabs my neck and tugs me toward him into a searing kiss. There's no warming up or getting our bearings—his tongue dives into my mouth, and I welcome the intrusion by matching his enthusiasm with my own. I press my body down into his, chasing each of his sexy noises with my mouth and wishing I'd taken the time to strip him completely.

No time like the present.

I break from his mouth and push up onto my knees, taking a moment to drink in his long form. Every dip of muscle, every bare stretch of brown skin, the light hair dusting the bottom of his abs and disappearing under his clothes.

His shorts are undone, hard cock pressing against his boxer briefs and trying to break free of the fly.

I'm actually about to do this.

To have sex with someone who isn't my wife, someone who I've known for way longer.

I've always been curious about how a man would feel, and I'm finally going to find out.

I lean in to kiss my way along Heath's chest and down his stomach. His skin is warm and salty, like nothing I've ever experienced, and when I reach his shorts, I shove them and his underwear out of the way in one go.

His cock slaps back against his abs, and before I have a moment to second-guess, I lean in and close my lips around him. Heath's gasp makes my cock throb. I suck him down, experimenting with the feel of him in my mouth. The scent, the taste, the sounds he's making … it's hot. So fucking hot.

I thought I'd be overly aware of the differences between a man and a woman, but there's no comparison. Obviously it's not the same, but the way my body is reacting to his is familiar. With one difference. This is so needy and primal and unique to Heath and him alone.

His balls are tight as I palm them, and when I glance up, I see the most familiar face in my world take on an expression I've never witnessed before.

His brown eyes are hooded, lips parted, normally styled hair a mess.

It makes me ache to kiss him again, to hold him close and enjoy the entire night wrapped around each other.

"Griff..."

I pull off his cock. "Yeah?"

"I want you to fuck me."

"What?"

"Well, I'd offer to fuck you, but we've already blown up your comfort zone enough for one night."

I crack a smile. "My blow job skills not up to scratch, huh?"

"There's no such thing as a bad blow job."

"I'll remember that." My gaze strays from his cock down his balls and to the swell of his ass. "So how do we do this?"

"Do you actually want to learn, or do you want me to do the work so we can get into it?"

"I should probably go with the first option, but my dick hurts."

Heath's familiar laugh warms my chest. "Lie down. We'll turn this into a tutorial."

He climbs off the bed and retrieves lube from his bedside. Then he plants one knee on the mattress and leans forward, holding on to the bottom bedpost as he exposes himself to me.

I lose track of what he's doing, only conscious of the click of the lube bottle and the sight of his tight hole. As soon as his slick fingers trail along his crease, I have to fist my cock to keep from coming.

"Just a warning," I say. "If I blow before I get inside you, we're going again."

"I'll hold you to that." Heath grins over his shoulder as he slides his first finger inside.

I let out a pathetic whimpery noise. Turns out no amount of porn could prepare me for the image of Heath bent over and fingering himself.

It's not until his second finger joins the first and he starts to stretch himself open that I realize he's watching me. We meet eyes, and that need to kiss him returns.

"You good?" he asks.

"Keep going." I don't sound like myself. "Please, don't stop."

"Wanna help?"

I scramble to my knees and close in behind him. "How?"

"Cover your fingers with lube, then press one in between mine."

I do exactly as he says, and when my finger is sliding into him, snug with the pressure sucking me inside, my head spins as I try to imagine that feeling around my cock.

Heath withdraws his fingers, so I press a second one inside him, then fit a third. "How is that?"

"Perfect, Griff. I'm ready."

No two words have ever sounded so sweet.

I grab the lube, cover my cock, then close in behind Heath. He's still bent over the bed, one foot on the floor and his knee on the mattress, putting his ass at the perfect height. My hand grabs his hip as I press my cock against his hole, preparing to push inside.

Heath grabs my wrist.

"At the risk of ruining the mood, you've only ever been with ... one person like this, right?"

"I've only ever been with one person, period."

"Well, I'm on PrEP and don't have anything—I get tested regularly. We don't need a condom, but just so you know, with anyone else—especially people you don't know —it's important."

Shit, I hadn't even thought about that.

I'm about to pull away when Heath releases my wrist and grabs my cock. "I trust you," he says. "If you want one, it's okay, but I'm happy to go without."

And I know, bone-deep, Heath would never do anything to hurt me. I lean in and brush a kiss against his lips. "I trust you more than anyone."

"Then hurry up and fuck me."

I'm gonna do my best.

Heath steadies himself against the bed as I grip my shaft and press forward. The head of my cock slips inside, and *shit*, it feels incredible. It's mind-blowing, but I'm determined to last. I might not be able to suck cock worth a damn, but I sure as hell can give him a pounding.

Just like my finger, his ass closes tight around me, the

pressure drawing me in deep. I try to go slow, but it's so hard to stay in control, and when Heath tilts his hips back, I slam home, bottoming out in one.

A long, satisfied moan comes from me. I've never experienced anything like this. The sight of his ass stretched to take my cock is the single most erotic moment of my life.

"I'm not going to last."

Heath laughs, and the slight tensing in his ass doesn't help the issue.

"Heath," I whine. "You're going to make me come before we even get started."

He straightens, hand reaching back to hold me against him. "Kiss me."

I dive in. His soft lips and strong tongue both drive me crazy and distract me enough from my dick that when I finally break from his mouth and attack his neck instead, I feel back in control again.

I give a small thrust, and every nerve in my body begs for more. Holy shit, I'm doing this. His body fits against mine perfectly, taking every thrust and meeting me with one of his own. From where I'm sucking on his shoulder, I can make out his cock bobbing in front of him. Red, hard, a tiny dot of precum appearing at the slit.

I throb at the sight and hold his hips tighter. Fingers bite into his skin, and the kisses I trail over his neck leave his skin raw and red. I'd worry about hurting him, but his babbled *yes* and *more* and *fuck* are all the green lights I need to keep going.

This moment is so surreal, so unlike anything I could

have ever imagined, and the arousal flooding my blood-stream is making it hard to keep check of reality.

Then Heath cards his fingers back through my hair. "Look at us." He gives me a tug, and I glance to the side he's pulling me toward.

My vision is hazy, but when I start to focus, I see exactly what he's talking about. We've left his wardrobe door open, and the mirror inside is tilted toward us.

It's a side view. Hot as hell. My thrusts slow down as I take in us together. His body is flush against mine, and from this angle, the difference in our size is more obvious. Him taller, me bulkier. But it's not his incredible body or his needy cock that I focus on; it's his face. If I thought that once the reality of fucking Heath sank in it would make things strange, I was wrong. Because seeing him like this makes me never want to stop.

I roll my hips, and he groans.

"*Griff.*" He reaches back to run a hand over my ass before squeezing it hard. "Do that again."

I give him what he needs, loving the way slowing down is keeping me turned on but off the edge. "Like that?"

"The way your body moves ... so hot."

I have no idea what he's talking about. Not when he's right in front of me. I hold his stare in the mirror and slowly drag my cock in and out, listening to every hitched breath and caught moan. I lean in and kiss his jaw, nip his ear, and run my lips over any skin within reach. I don't drop eye contact the whole time. I need it.

The reminder that it's him and me is making this a thousand times more intense than I ever imagined a one-night stand could be.

And as much as I want this to last all night, I really need to come.

I close my arms around him to thrust harder, and this time he lets a "*nrgh*" slip out. An appreciative sound rumbles in my chest, but it isn't loud enough to cover the sounds of my hips hitting his ass, the steady slap getting gradually faster as Heath stops holding back.

The familiar scents of his shampoo and sweat are all around me, and when I let my gaze slip from his face to his cock, seeing how hard he is pushes me to the edge.

"You need to come," I gasp.

My arms tighten around him, pulling him down onto my cock with every thrust. The pressure, his hand working himself in time with our bodies, the checked-out expression on his face ... then the cry he lets out as his whole body tenses and he comes.

Each pulse of his cock has my balls tightening, drawing up, desperate to unload. His eyes have fallen closed as his strokes turn lazy, but I need more.

"Look at me."

His eyes flick open, and the satisfaction in them makes me want to bury my face in his shoulder and live there. Instead, I force myself not to break contact as I drive into him, harder and harder, tipping closer to the edge until a ripple races from my spine to my balls and my whole body shudders while I unload into him.

For a couple of moments, I hold him to me, catching my breath and letting what happened between us settle.

"You okay?" he asks, breaking the stillness of the room.

And with all the happy vibes pumping through my body, my smile and answer are genuine. "Incredible."

Chapter Seventeen

HEATH

When I wake up with Griff's heavy arm over my back, I let my eyes fall closed again. Partly because I want to burn last night into my memories, and partly because I don't want to face today.

No matter how you look at it, I fucked up.

Years and years of friendship all boiled over last night to possibly the greatest pounding I've ever experienced. My whole body yearns to press into his side and stay there for the rest of today, to ask Griff to stay and maybe have another round, but as hot as that experience was, it was *Griff*.

I can't stop my eyes from opening again to look at him.

He looks so peaceful sleeping. That concentration line across his forehead is missing, and he looks so much younger without it. Still, even having him asleep next to me doesn't make it any easier to digest that my oldest friend fucked me into oblivion last night.

I think ... I think I'm freaking out.

Which makes me freak out more because ... why?

It was only sex. I've been the one flirting with him, saying it wouldn't mean anything, and I believed that would be the case. I've hooked up with friends before—kinda hard not to in a town like Kilborough, and it didn't change anything. We traded orgasms and then went out for brunch the next day like it was nothing.

Actually ... I don't think I have a friend I haven't slept with at some point. Some of them multiple times.

Except Griff.

Nearly my whole sexual life, he's been in a relationship, completely off-limits. It's never been an issue because I haven't wanted him like that, and I thought I never would. What we have ... I'd be lying if I said he isn't the most important person in my world. With those other friendships, if they had ended it would have sucked, but I would have been fine.

If I've fucked things up with Griff ... My heart squeezes.

Yeah, no. That's not an option.

I flop onto my back and cover my face with my hands. I need to play this cool, exactly like I do with every other one of my hookups. There's no reason why this should be any different.

Except it's *Griff*.

My throat feels thick when I push myself out of bed and grab a clean pair of briefs. I sneak out of my bedroom without waking him, take a piss, then head to the kitchen and put the coffee machine on.

I figure a coffee and some time to think is all I need, but I've barely poured myself a mug when Griff walks out. He's wearing the clothes he showed up in before we went out yesterday, along with a guarded expression.

"Morning," I say, forcing a confidence that hasn't caught up with me yet.

"Hey ..." He glances toward the door before pulling out a stool at the counter. "How are you ... you know."

"I always feel great after sex. Tea?"

"Thanks."

I make him one, and the silence that settles in between us isn't comfortable. As much as I want to avoid the issue, I ask, "Are *you* okay?"

"I think so." He frowns. "I can't shake the thought that I've just cheated though."

"I get that."

He drops his gaze to his cup. "I hate it. Last night was ..." A heavy exhale rushes out of him. "Fucking incredible, Heath. I don't want to think that way. I want to focus on us and how amazing it was, but ..."

The obvious pain in his voice makes me want to comfort him like I normally would, but I stay standing where I am. "Yeah?"

"We can't tell her." His voice sounds wrecked.

"Poppy?"

His eyes meet mine, and he nods. "We're not together, so

I know it wasn't cheating, but I'd hate if she thought I was waiting for things to end so we could get together."

And just like that, I'm feeling the same guilt he is. "She'd assume there was more to it than friendship all these years."

"Exactly."

"Fuck." I run my hand through my hair, trying to settle my thoughts. At the end of the day, realistically, I know Poppy has no say in what happens between Griff and me, but I care about her too, and I don't want to hurt anyone. I swallow and force myself to relax because there's a very simple answer to all of this. "There's no reason why she'd need to know," I say.

"What do you mean?"

"Well, it was only sex. A one-time thing. It doesn't change anything between us. Chalk it up to a learning experience." Who am I trying to convince here?

He watches me for a moment, and it hits me that I don't know *what* he's thinking. That's ... new. I don't like it.

"You're right," Griff says. He has a long drink of his tea before rounding the counter and rinsing his mug. I watch him open the dishwasher and set it on the rack before turning to me. "Thanks for the learning experience."

"Anything for you." Somehow those words hold more weight than I intended.

"So, I'll, uh, see you at work tomorrow?"

"Of course."

Griff grabs his wallet and phone and goes to head for the front door, but before he can make it halfway, I close the distance and catch his arm.

"We're okay, right?" I feel compelled to ask. "Everything is fine."

Griff's intense blue stare sweeps over my face, and my goddamn cock hasn't got the message because it perks up at the way he's looking at me.

"Please say yes," I whisper.

His sweet half smile jumps onto his face. "We're always okay." He leans up and brushes a soft kiss against my cheek. I want to hold him there, make him linger. "I meant it when I said last night was incredible."

"Yeah. It really was."

He watches me, and I can't bring myself to look away. "We got it out of our system at least. No more flirting."

"Right. That's exactly what this was." But fuck, if he took me back to bed right now, I'd be moaning his name in minutes. Dammit, no. My cock needs to get the memo that we're one and done. Before I can stop myself, I lean in and press a hard kiss to his lips. I give him a second, wait to see if he does anything about it, before I reluctantly pull away. "I always kiss my hookups goodbye."

"Right." He swallows. "Bye."

Then he pulls his arm from my grip and leaves.

I don't feel right, not with everything so up in the air. The awkwardness between us wasn't normal, and now I'm left with this gross feeling in my gut that won't shift. What is happening to me?

So Griffin gave me the hottest sex in a long, long time. Maybe ever. So what that the eye contact made everything so much more intense? And who cares that my heart is actually in pain at the thought things might change between us now?

I blow out a breath and grip the countertop. This freak-out will pass. And quickly. No matter what I'm feeling at the moment, it doesn't matter. Poppy doesn't deserve to get hurt, and I wouldn't strain her relationship with Griff—or, fuck, his with Felix—for anything in the world.

We should have thought this through more.

Though, if I'm honest, I doubt it would have made a difference. The moment Griff pulled me onto the dance floor with him, maybe even before, I'd known where the night was going, and there wasn't a single part of me that wanted to put on the brakes.

For Griff, I'm sure the answer would have been different. He's put off a relationship and even hooking up to try to keep his family happy, and if us having anything more than friendship could risk that, there's no way he'd do it a second time.

So I need to support him. No more sex? Done. Keeping it quiet? Easy.

Last night was a tiny blip on the timeline, a slight deviation from our friendship, but with us both on the same page, we can get back on track.

Before I do anything, I walk back into my bedroom and strip the bed, then shove the sheets—along with the smell of him and sex—into the washing machine.

After that, I grab my keys and head out.

Mom usually goes to church first thing in the morning,

but thanks to my sleep-in, by the time I get to her place, she's already home and in her garden.

Her face lights up when I pull into her driveaway and climb out.

"And here I was thinking I'd make it a whole weekend without you checking up on me."

I give her a sheepish smile before jogging up onto the porch. She's slower to stand, stiffer. I try to ignore it and pull her into a hug. "Is it a crime to visit you now?"

"Of course not." She pulls away. "But I'm not an obligation either."

"I know. I just wanted to take you to lunch."

She shakes her head. "I can't, I'm afraid. I have to get these moth orchids repotted, and the garden bed around the side is being attacked by weeds."

"Mind if I help?"

Mom hesitates. "There's no one else you'd rather be spending your Sunday with?"

"Don't talk nonsense."

"Heath ..." She turns a sympathetic look on me, eyes the exact shape and shade as mine. "I'm worried about you."

"There's no need to be."

"You're forty-three. And still single."

Why did I think that coming here would make me feel any better? I sigh and scrub my hand through my hair. "This is the last thing I want to talk about."

"Why? Is there someone?"

I hate how excited she sounds about that. And that I

have to let her down. "No. There's no one. I'm just getting tired of telling people that I like being single."

"I know, I know. I get it. The independence and whatever. But ... even though he's gone, I wouldn't change my time with your father for anything. And I worry about you not finding that same person for you."

Thoughts of Griff immediately fill my mind, and there I go failing at forgetting about him again. But ... well, taking sex away from it, Griff ticks the boxes of what I'd expect a life partner to do. He's loyal to a fault, loves me, is always there to listen when I need him to. He doesn't try to hide who he is deep down with me, and I never feel the need to do that with him either.

And that's exactly why I can't lose him.

"I've already found that person," I tell her. "Griff."

"Friends don't count."

"Why don't they? You always say you married your best friend. And look at Griff and Poppy. They're about to be divorced, so clearly the marriage thing isn't permanent. But what we have is. We might not do everything husbands *do*" —well, *again*—"but he covers off everything else for me."

"I suppose ..." she grudgingly concedes.

"Then let's stop focusing on me and get those orchids into their new homes."

And pray it helps distract me enough to forget the little swoop in my gut every time I think about Griff.

Chapter Eighteen

GRIFF

I spend all day Sunday sitting on my porch, drinking soda and working on my chairs. By the afternoon, they're put together and solid, and I've sanded them both back, ready to stain. It's the perfect day. Nothing fills me with satisfaction the way working with my hands does.

Nothing except—*nope*. I'm refusing to think about it.

I've kept busy and I've been good, and I definitely have *not* been picturing Heath's face last night while I drove into him.

Fuck. I think I lasted thirty minutes that time? Time to reset the clock again and find another distraction. I move the chairs inside until I have time to seal the wood and am contemplating making a start on the table when my phone rings.

My gut flips out at the thought of Heath calling me, but when I check the display, it's someone else entirely.

I'm both ridiculously happy and guarded as I answer my son's call. "Ah, remembered your old man, did you?"

Felix sniggers. "At least you called yourself it before I could."

There's something about hearing his voice that buoys me. It's like armor. Knowing Felix is happy means nothing else can get to me. "Old and distinguished. You could be so lucky."

"By the time I reach old age, I'll be rich, and it won't matter what I look like because everyone will want me for my money."

There's a ninety percent chance he's teasing, but still a ten percent chance he's serious. "I'm so glad I taught you priorities."

"And about the important things in life. If it wasn't for you, my goals would be much lower. Instead, I'm going to be the next Hugh Hefner. But with better hair."

"How do you even know who he is?"

"Playboy, duh."

"You—wait, no, I don't want to know. Do you want to put me in an early grave?" It doesn't stop me from querying my son's sexuality again though. He talks about girls a lot and now ... Playboy? But I've sensed crushes before on boys and could have sworn I glimpsed something on his computer that I never needed to know about my son. But he's in college. And we've supported him in everything.

Surely if he was bi like me, he would have said something ... even though I've never actually mentioned it to him.

He laughs. "How are you both doing?"

"Good." Somehow I keep my voice even, because it's not technically a lie. "But you didn't call to be filled in on your boring parents. How is college?"

And like I'd hoped, Felix launches into detailed stories of his classes, his dorm and the guy he shares the room with, along with the party he went to last night.

"I hope you weren't drinking," I say, as though my night was completely innocent.

"No, no. Me? Of course not."

"Good answer." He's eighteen and living away from home. I'm not an idiot. I know he'll drink. But before he left, we made sure to have a very frank conversation with him about knowing your limits, alcohol poisoning, and not getting anyone pregnant.

As much as I'm sure he's making *some* bad choices, I also know Felix is a smart kid and can look out for himself.

Which hurts.

Because up until now, he relied on me. He needed me. He doesn't anymore.

Which should be freeing because I get to live a different type of life now, but ... I'll never have that again.

Felix finishes his monologue. "Hey, can you throw Mom on?"

Oh, fuck. The guilt of betraying him cuts deep, and I don't answer for a second. "Ah, she's ... out. Maybe give her phone a call?"

"Nah, I won't bug her. When she gets home, just let her know I'll be in all night."

It's on the tip of my tongue to tell him that she won't be coming home, at least not to me, but how do I bring him down when he's happy and doing well at school? When he's settled and thinks life is sweet and his parents are happy?

Well, we are happy. Maybe more than we have been in a long time, just not in the way he thinks.

"Love you, Dad."

I've missed my chance. "Love you too, kiddo."

We hang up, and like that, I can't avoid the knot of guilt in my gut anymore. What would he think of me, finding out I'd slept with "Uncle Heath"? He doesn't know I'm bi. He doesn't know a lot of things.

Shit.

I run a hand over my face and text Poppy to call Felix. When she replies she will, I respond with, *Once you're done, I think we need to talk.*

Heath doesn't show up on Monday morning to steal my coffee like he did every day last week. Instead, when I'm struggling into a work shirt that feels almost suffocating, there's a knock on my front door.

It's after eight, which means Heath is definitely working and not just being polite, so I assume Poppy is here early.

"Hey," I say, opening the door and letting her in.

Her reddish-brown hair is pulled back in a ponytail, and she's dressed for work. Unlike me, she looks right at home in managing a resort. She and Heath have that in common.

Fuck.

Heath.

Nope. I cannot think of him while talking to my ex-wife.

"Not going to offer me a drink?" she asks, amusement in her voice.

"Ah. Yeah. Sorry. Do you want something?"

"Water is fine." She looks around, and her gaze snags on the dying flowers on the counter. "You know if you bought fake ones, you wouldn't have to worry about the mess they make."

I give her a placid smile because we've been having this discussion for years. She hated real flowers in the house, but fake ones are so ... depressing.

She moves to settle on the couch. "Are you okay?"

"Yeah, good." I pour us both a water and join her.

"You seem stressed."

That's putting it lightly. After all, why would I be stressed about lying to my kid and sleeping with our friend —and that even though I know it'll hurt them ... I want to do it again? I'm a selfish asshole.

"I don't feel right lying to Felix."

"What?" She looks around. "I thought we were settled on this. We'll tell him about us on his first visit home."

She's right; we had decided, but that's still a month away, and another month of lying to Felix is going to kill me. "I'm worried about blindsiding him. Maybe we should have been up-front from the start?"

"Griff ..."

I force myself to look at her.

"He's an adult now. We did what we did so he could focus on school, and he graduated with high scores in nearly every class. We both know Felix would have worked himself up over the divorce and wouldn't have been able to concentrate on schoolwork. If we'd told him and stayed living together, he would have been distracted trying to parent trap us, and if you moved out, it would have been too much upheaval. We made the right choice."

Deep down, I know she's right. We gave him the best childhood we could. But I can't shake the feeling he's going to find out from someone else, and then he'll refuse to speak to either of us. With him across the other side of the country, I won't even be able to confront him.

"What if someone finds out we're living apart? And it gets back to him?"

"How?" she asks. "Most of his school friends left for college too, and it's not like he's here to overhear something in the diner."

"What if one of his friends' parents find out and they mention it to their kid, who mentions it to—"

Poppy sighs. "You're making this into a bigger deal than it needs to be. No one is gossiping about us—it's not as though we're out there publicly dating and hanging off other people. You work here. Most people probably haven't realized we're living apart."

I take a deep breath. "Okay, yeah, you're right." I've always been someone who keeps mostly to himself and his small circle of friends, and while Poppy is far more social than I am, we're not gossip-worthy in this town.

I hope.

Poppy stays until we're supposed to start work, and we talk about her trip back from California since we haven't had a chance to with all the business talk. It's nice to catch up. It's also nice to have an easy conversation with her and confirm my feelings are completely platonic.

And I mean *platonic* platonic, not *Heath* platonic.

Even thinking his name sends jitters through me. I glance over at Poppy, wondering if I should say anything.

We both knew that separating would mean moving on, and I made it no secret how desperate I was to have sex again. But still ... will it be too soon for her? She's a practical person, so maybe not. It's who I took that step with that will catch her off guard.

Through our whole relationship, Heath was there for everything. He joined us on double dates when we were younger; he was the one I told as soon as I lost my virginity, as soon as I planned to propose, and as soon as we were talking about trying for a baby. He was my best man. Felix's godfather. He's around for most holidays, usually stops by over the weekends, and he and Poppy work side by side most days while I'm off doing my thing. They business plan together and grab lunch together.

I run my hand over my face to try and hide my thoughts. It doesn't work.

"There's something else on your mind," Poppy says.

"Nope."

"Okay, keep your secrets. I'm going to say, though, if you have some kind of internal angst over sex or seeing someone else, don't. Whatever you do is none of my business anymore. I'll just remind you that we need to be discreet until Felix knows we've split." She gets up, and like she can't stop herself, she goes to clean the kitchen. The looks she throws my way when she finds unrinsed dishes in the sink are easy enough to ignore, but when she grabs the dying flowers and dumps them in the bin, it makes me frown.

Her words should fill me with relief. She's right. It's none of her business. And if I'd chosen one of those faceless men I was dancing with the other night, I wouldn't have a problem.

I should have picked up a total random and moved on.

But I picked Heath.

On purpose.

Seeing the way he was watching me from the bar filled me with the kind of want I've never experienced before. Even remembering it now is causing an awkward situation.

The second I left those men to approach him, I knew what I was doing.

I knew what I wanted.

The problem is, once wasn't enough.

I'm not going to prove Heath right though. It's possible for me to have sex and not expect more. These feelings are a pain in the ass for right now, but they'll fade because that's what feelings do.

Until then, I just need to keep a bit of distance. I don't like it—having him not show up today didn't sit right—but it's probably what we need.

As long as our friendship survives.

Which it will.

It has to.

Chapter Nineteen

HEATH

The decision not to see Griff this morning was a hard one, but I think it was for the best. Since yesterday morning, we haven't had any contact, which isn't unusual, but I felt the space more acutely than I ever have before.

I meant what I said to Mom. Griff is my person. I'll do whatever I have to in order to protect what we have with my life, but after this distance, I don't think space is something I can give him. I'm way too on edge waiting for any sign of him to show up at work that when I do my walk around to check in on everything, my feet take me dangerously close to the turnoff to his place. Somehow, I convince myself to keep walking.

His presence feels like it's reeling me in.

The best thing I can do is go on pretending like everything is normal and he didn't give me the best dicking out of my life.

Griff and Poppy are already in the back office when I get to reception. I can hear their voices in the hall as I pause by Michelle at the reception desk to make sure everything is covered.

Unfortunately, there are no world-ending dilemmas, so I take a deep breath and head back there too.

Poppy barely looks up from the computer she's working at when she sends a "morning" in my direction, but Griff's focus immediately snaps to mine. He doesn't say anything even as his cheeks darken.

I look away before Poppy can pick up on anything because Griff is not being subtle.

"Good morning." Somehow, my voice is steady, even with the rush of emotions plaguing me.

I can feel Griff watching me, but I don't look at him again. If he's thinking something inappropriate or if there are any signs of regret, I don't want to know. I'm a professional who is thinking only professional thoughts.

"Last week, I think I covered everything," Poppy says, finishing up whatever she's doing on the computer. "So I thought starting from this week, I'm going to be more hands-off. The two of you can work together on things, and I'll be here for support if you need me, but, Heath, you know our systems as well as I do." She gives Griff a small smile. "I think you should shadow Heath for the next few days. He has more contact with our staff and the guests, and he knows how everything should be run."

"Ah, I, umm—"

"Too easy," I say before Griff's stuttering draws attention. "If I show him what my day to day looks like, we can come up with a plan for who covers what."

"Excellent." She stands up and grabs her laptop. "I'm going to work in the restaurant if you need me. The less hands-on I am, the better, but if you need anything, make sure you reach out. I'm available."

She leaves, unaware of whatever there is growing between me and Griff. And thank fuck for that. Things cannot return to normal soon enough.

I prop myself against the desk next to where he's sitting. "So, where should we start? I just got back from my walk around, but I can take you—"

"Goddamn," he mutters.

"Come again?"

Griff looks me over, and he swallows. It unsettles my already sensitive nerves. I'm like a live wire, sparking and fizzling, waiting for Griff to set me alight.

Instead, he looks away. "I'm happy to follow your lead."

"In more ways than one." It's a risk, hinting at what happened and making a joke out of it, but when Griff glances up in time to see me wink, the seriousness he's been holding on to melts, and a smile slips out.

"I don't think I can talk about it yet."

"Talk about what?" I feign ignorance. "I was talking about work. Where is your filthy mind at?"

He laughs and stands, bringing his body uncomfortably close to mine. "You're going to be the death of me."

"Only if you take everything so seriously."

"You're right." This time, *he* winks, and I almost melt. "Your ass looks good in those pants."

Hearing him joke about this has me so fucking happy, I want to tug his earlobe, but I can't risk touching him. "Careful, Griff. I'm your employee. That could be taken as harassment."

"The only power imbalance between us is that if you walk out and leave me, this whole place will tank. You never need to be worried about your job."

Yikes. Way to guilt-trip me without even realizing it. He's right though. Without Poppy, I'm basically stuck here. Might as well resign myself to that fact now.

It's not like that job ever got back to me anyway.

Griff's vibrant blue eyes don't look as guarded as they did when I first walked in. All I can sense in them is affection and contentment, two things we've always had with each other.

Do not flirt back, do not flirt back.

My mouth doesn't listen. "In that case, I probably shouldn't tell you your ass looks good in those pants either?"

"You definitely shouldn't."

"Then I *really* shouldn't tell you that it looked even better ... *not* in those pants."

He groans and steps back. "We're not talking about that."

I mime locking my lips.

"I'm serious, Heath. It can't happen again."

"Did I say anything about wanting it to happen again?"

He levels me with a stare. "Don't you?"

I look away. This is the part where I remind him it was only sex. That I'm not him and don't get attached to every man I sleep with. The problem is, we were already attached, and since Saturday, I've had a growing ache in my chest that I can't shift. "I understand the situation," I say instead. "We both know nothing good would come from a repeat."

"Thank you."

He doesn't call me out on avoiding his question, just like I don't ask him the same one. Whether we want it to happen again or not, it can't. What's the point in torturing ourselves over it?

"Maybe we can go out again on the weekend and do things properly this time?" I suggest.

He makes a noncommitted noise and gestures to the door. "Should we ..."

"Work. Yes." The thing we're both here for.

We work side by side up until lunchtime, when Griff ducks out on me. I have no idea where he disappears to, but when our break ends, he's not in the office. Maybe he's avoiding me? Or maybe calling out sick to avoid the things he's supposed to be learning?

Either way, I head for his place, planning to drag him back to work through any means necessary.

I find him where he usually is, on his porch, whistling as he carves into a chunk of wood. He doesn't notice me at first, and I take a moment to watch him in his element. He's got his shirt off and his pants rolled up to his knees—something I wish I could do with how hot it is outside—and he seems ... happy. Griff isn't made for office work.

Ignoring the view of his thick arms and barrel chest, I step off the path and around the flowers obscuring me from sight. Griff's bright blue eyes meet mine, and he sends me a smile before going back to what he's doing.

At least his body language doesn't look like he's avoiding me.

"What is that?" I ask.

"Eh. Just me fucking around. Maybe making something." He continues to chip away at the wood.

I sit down next to him and watch for a moment. "Something for me?"

He doesn't look my way, but I catch his shifts in expression. "Where would this piece of shit fit in your fancy apartment?"

"Anywhere," I tell him. "It might not match, but that doesn't mean it won't fit."

"I'm out of practice, so it might not be any good."

"Even better."

He chuckles. "You're not making sense."

"It could be the most indistinguishable hunk of junk, and I'd love it anyway because it would remind me that you're back to doing something you love."

"Someone's sounding kinda mushy."

"Only kinda?"

He nudges me. "You're gonna make me blush."

And if he thinks that would dissuade me, he clearly

doesn't know me at all. But where my first reaction is to keep pushing, I let him off the hook.

"You know we were supposed to be back like ten minutes ago?"

"Ah, oops," he says, going to put down what he's working on, but I reach out and grab his hand.

"A long lunch today isn't going to kill us."

"It won't?"

I shake my head and after a brief pause ask, "Can you teach me?"

His mouth drops for a second, but he quickly brushes off his surprise as he hands the wood and carving knife over. "Of course. Here."

I look down at them, trying to figure out where to start. Griff hasn't bothered to do much more than strip the bark away, but I turn to the side he was working on and hack at the wood.

His warm chuckle fills the air before he wraps his arms around me.

"Like this." The low voice in my ear sends jitters through my stomach. He holds me close as he takes my hands, and if he thinks I'm going to be able to concentrate on anything more than how he's touching me, he's even more clueless than I thought.

Griff adjusts my hold, then steers my hand through the motions. The heat from his body is seeping through my shirt, and it doesn't sound like either of us is breathing.

I forget to watch what I'm doing and turn my gaze to

Griff's face instead. It's so close I can make out every hair of his stubble, every tiny line that creases his lips.

The memory of how his mouth felt on mine hits hard and fast. Us, in the mirror, positioned similar to how we are now. His big arms holding me close ... his front pressed to my back ...

Griff looks up suddenly, and the eye contact makes my cock react. His face reflects the heat burning in my gut back at me, and my hands tighten on the knife and wood to stop myself from dropping those and grabbing him.

"Heath ..." His husky rasp is unfair. It threatens to unravel me.

My self-control is usually grade A, but apparently when it comes to him, I lose all semblance of control.

Somehow, he's closer. And closer again.

I'm not sure which of us moved, but I can smell the mint on his breath, the scent of his sweat, feel the warm puff of air as it hits my lips.

Then my grip on the wood slips and—

"Mother*fucker*!"

Griff launches to his feet and takes two wide paces before bending forward.

"Are you ..."

"Towel ... ice ... something." His voice is strained, and when he turns around, there's blood pouring from between his fingers.

Fuck.

I drop what I'm holding, then spring up and race inside,

grabbing a bag of peas from the freezer and towel, then take them both outside.

Griff's whole body is tense with pain, and as soon as I pass the towel over, he wraps it around his hand.

"What happened?" I ask.

"You fucking stabbed me."

DMC Group Chat

Art: *Heard you were stabbed.*

Payne: *Please tell me this is an analogy for something?*

Griff: *Nah, I'm at the doctors now. It was only a nick though.*

Orson: *Shit, are you okay? Do you need anything?*

Griff: *A new best friend?*

Art: *In Heath's defense, haven't we all wanted to stab our friends at some point?*

Payne: *Ahhh no?*

Orson: *I just remembered, I can't make the next DMC meeting.*

Griff: *If I've already been stabbed, does that mean I'm safe now?*

Payne: *Or you're so irritating it's likely to happen again?*

Art: *I think it depends.*

Griff: *On?*

Art: *Whether this was a sex thing.*

Griff: *Of course you'd go there! Though, actually ... kinda?*

Payne: *Wot!*

Art: *What????*

Orson: *We really, really don't need to know.*

Chapter Twenty

GRIFF

Well, that's one way to put an end to something that definitely shouldn't be happening.

I grit my teeth as Estelle puts two stitches in my middle finger. I have no idea how Heath managed it, but we're lucky he didn't slice off the tip.

What's a few days of discomfort to avoid a big mistake?

And *damn* it would have been a mistake, but I'd wanted it. Badly. The way my body has been reacting to Heath's isn't something I'm proud of but doesn't seem to be something I can get under control either.

I was right that avoiding him is the safest option, but he obviously doesn't want to play it that way. Neither do I ... not really. Life doesn't feel right without Heath in it. But when I can't be around him without wanting to peel that suit off him, what am I supposed to do?

And when I get back home, expecting him to be gone for the day, he's waiting on my front porch, jacket off and shirt unbuttoned. I have a feeling with how hot it is that he would have removed it completely if things weren't already so weird.

"How is it?" He nods to my hand, a hint of guilt in his tone.

"Fine. Only a little nick."

Heath snorts but doesn't argue. It had looked bad before he dropped me off, but now that it's clean and not bleeding, it's hard to see what the big deal was about.

He doesn't apologize, which is a relief because he only did it about a thousand times before I left. It's on the tip of my tongue to invite him in for dinner, like I normally would, but if I'm serious about getting over this *thing*, I need to ignore everything I'd normally do and remember that my family comes first.

"Here to check up on me?" I cross my arms, careful of my finger, and lean against the side of the house.

"I'm the one who went slasher on you, so I thought the least I could do was stop by and cook you dinner."

Flutters hit my gut that have no right to be there. "Thanks, but I have leftovers from last night."

I see the exact moment what I'm saying clicks with him. "Well, good. Wouldn't want them to go to waste."

"Exactly."

He licks his lips, then forces a smile as he stands. "I'll see you bright and early tomorrow, then."

"Sounds good."

As soon as he leaves, the unsettled feeling from yesterday returns. We've never been through something like this before. Most friends fight, and while we've had disagreements before, we've never had something like this, where it feels like our dynamic has been irreversibly changed, and I don't know how to fix it.

All from one night together. One orgasm. Was it worth it?

The flood of butterflies that hits me when I think about holding him, pleasuring him, makes me want to say yes.

If things were different, if I didn't have to think of Poppy and Felix, and if I thought Heath might actually be looking for more than sex, then maybe those butterflies would be correct. Maybe it would be the thing to take a friendship as strong as ours and turn it into more.

I look around my house, reminding myself that this was my fresh start. The page was clean, and my life was mine to build up to whatever I wanted it to be. Simple was my only aim, so how is everything so much more complicated than when I was stuck in a failed marriage?

I need to get back on track. To remind myself of the quiet and happy life I was picturing when I moved out. Running the resort wasn't a part of that, but it looks like I have no say in the matter, so the other stress—wanting to fuck Heath again despite knowing the massive explosion it could cause—is what I can fix.

I can't ignore him, even though I probably should. It's too painful to contemplate. So, new rule: I avoid all attempts at flirting and being alone. I will keep things work focused, which will hopefully stop me from being a total failure there.

I need to look at the big picture.

Getting past this, back to friends, and making sure Poppy and Felix are none the wiser.

I'm regretting not letting him cook me dinner though, because the leftovers were a bullshit excuse, and I can't be bothered putting together anything. After checking my cupboards, it's not even a question of *want*. There's no food here. Yet another thing I need to get better at organizing.

I guess I never realized how much Poppy did for me.

I text Art to meet me at Killer Brew, grab my keys, and leave.

The road out of the resort meets up with the one that leads to the prison, and by looking left toward it, I can tell it's another busy night. The whole ghost town and Kill Pen are lit up like a spaceship, even though the summer tourist season is technically over. It's a little quieter, but with Halloween less than two months away, our business will stay steady until then.

Art hasn't texted back by the time I pull up in the Kilborough Brewery parking lot, so I climb out of my car, pass through the bar area inside, and climb the stairs behind the bar to where his office is. There's every chance he's gone home, but I'm hopeful.

The light in his office fills the hall, only once I reach the door, I find he's not alone. The bartender who's always flirting with him is sitting on the side of his desk, leaning in, while Art eyes him darkly from his chair.

I knock on the doorframe. "Am I interrupting?"

"Nope," Art says, not taking his eyes off ... I think it's Joey?

Joey glances at me over his shoulder, cocky smirk in place. "I was just telling Art I need the weekend off for a wedding, and he was being *so* accommodating by letting me work tomorrow morning instead."

"If accommodating is asking for your resignation, then I was being exactly that."

Joey tilts his head. "You have an odd way of flirting, *Mr.* de Almeida."

"I've never had a complaint before." Art stands suddenly so he's looming over Joey. "But considering I'm not flirting with you, I can see how you'd be confused."

Instead of being deterred, Joey slowly stands too. "So ... I'll see you tomorrow."

Art glares, but Joey's smile gets bigger.

"See? That's why you're everyone's favorite boss." Joey winks at me as he leaves. "Total teddy bear."

I wait until he disappears before I turn to Art and pin him with a look. "What was that?"

"A pain in my ass."

"I feel like I witnessed something dirty. Why am I craving a scotch and a smoke?"

"Because you have a filthy mind."

"I honestly have no idea how you haven't caved yet. He's gorgeous."

Art waves a hand toward the door. "Have at it."

"Sorry to say he has no interest in anyone but you."

"And the different women he takes home each night."

I shrug and pull out the chair opposite him. "I would have done him already." Would I actually though? It feels like what I'm supposed to say. Joey *is* hot. And clearly flirty guys are my style, but I'm struggling to let go of Heath and focus on anything else.

"Good thing you're not in my position, then," Art says. "Because he only does it when he wants something. There's no actual intent behind it."

"And if there was?"

"I'd bend him over my desk and have my way with the bastard."

I burst out laughing. "So him being your employee doesn't worry you?"

"Nothing worries me." He narrows his dark-rimmed eyes. "Why do you ask?"

"No reason."

"It's Heath, isn't it?"

My head drops back. "On a scale of one to Beau-having-the-hots-for-Payne, how obvious am I?"

"Smack bang in the middle."

"Fuck. How did you know?"

"Part of it was assuming you guys would bang at some point, and ... I dunno. There's always been this connection, I guess. You're both so comfortable and in sync with each other."

"Because we were friends."

"And how's that working out for you?" Art chuckles. "Has anything happened?"

"We slept together last weekend."

"Was it good?"

Good? That doesn't even begin to cover it. "It was ... hell, Art. I don't think I'll ever beat it. I've never had that type of chemistry with someone. I know I don't have a lot of experience, but I don't see how anything can match that intensity."

"Chemistry isn't something you should take for granted."

I point my thumb back over my shoulder. "Like you can talk."

"We're not discussing him. Now, let me guess, you want a repeat?"

"Badly, but I can't."

"Why?"

"Lots of reasons. Our friendship, for one. And it would be too weird for Poppy and Felix if Heath and I started seeing each other."

"Ah, it's not just sex?"

As much as I wish it was, there's no point lying to Art. "Not for me."

"Then why are you holding back? You're getting divorced; Poppy no longer has a say in your life."

"She doesn't, but she's Felix's mom. We need to have a

relationship, and if I start seeing Heath, it could be uncomfortable for her. Plus, *Felix* ... I don't even want to know how he'll react."

"Haven't you put his feelings first enough?"

"He's my *son*. That's not an eighteen-year job."

Art's quiet for a moment. "How does Heath feel about it?"

"Your guess is as good as mine. I mean, he's as flirty as ever, but even if he did want to hook up again, I can't risk my family and our friendship for sex. It's not worth it."

"Can't have been as earth-shattering as you thought, then." Art grins. "Fine. If nothing can happen, you move on. It's not hard."

"Unlike you, we're not all emotionless voids."

"*Hey.*" He pretends to be offended, but I can tell he's not. "I'm just good at prioritizing. Letting the darkness into your soul is bad chakra."

"Uh ... what?"

"Dunno. I think I heard it in a movie once."

"Okay." He somehow exasperates and endears me with every conversation. "So how do I get over him?"

"I'll take you out this weekend. We'll fuck all these feelings out, and you'll start next week as a new man."

I narrow my eyes. "Just what feelings do *you* have to fuck out?"

"None. I'm an emotionless void, remember?"

His tone is convincing. Maybe *too* convincing. "Fine. Take me out. And make sure I don't try to sleep with you."

"I'd laugh, but I have the suspicion that's exactly what happened with Heath."

"It is."

"Hmm ..."

"What?"

Art drums his fingers on the desk. "I think you should tell him where your head is at. Give him honesty. You two have always had that kind of relationship, and it's a beautiful thing."

"And scare him off from even wanting to be around me? He said I couldn't handle a one-night stand."

"Yeah, but what you had with him wasn't a one-night stand. It wasn't casual. The two of you have far too much history for that to ever be a thing. And whether it makes him uncomfortable or not, once you've moved past it, he'll respect you for telling him."

"Or never speak to me again."

"What's life without a little gamble?"

Except gambling with the most important thing in my life—aside from Felix—isn't a smart move.

I put an end to the Heath conversation, and we head downstairs for dinner.

It's not until later, when I get back from Killer Brew, that I pull out my phone, gather the limited courage I have in my arsenal, and text Heath. As much as I hate it, Art is right about honesty.

Am I taking the coward's way out? Of course.

Because if I hear his voice, I might cave.

Me: *I keep thinking about today.*

179

It's not what I meant to say, but I hit Send anyway.

Heath: *Your best friend attacking you would leave an impression.*

Me: *And yet, it's not the part I was talking about.*

Heath: *So ... it wasn't just in my head? What I thought almost happened actually almost happened?*

Me: *It did.*

Heath: *Shit.*

Me: *Yeah. I fucked up.*

Heath: *Sorry to storm your pity party, but you weren't the only one there.*

Me: *I know but ... I said I could do the casual thing and I don't think I can.*

Heath: *Why?*

Me: *Because I want you. Again. So fucking badly.*

I shouldn't be telling him any of this, but I've never kept anything from Heath before, and I can't start now.

Me: *I know I shouldn't, and I know it would have been different if I'd hooked up with one of those other men, but ... I couldn't.*

Heath: *Want to know a secret?*

Me: *We don't have secrets.*

Heath: *I'm glad you chose me.*

My breath catches, and something aches so deep in my chest, I almost give in and call him.

Me: *I hear incompetence is a turn on for some.*

Heath: *Nah, Griff ... it was all you.*

I have to set my phone down for a second. The only thing harder than being honest with him that I want more is him echoing some of what I'm feeling back at me. I need to get on top of it.

Me: *We can't do this.*

Heath: *I know.*

Me: *The problem is, I don't know how to be around you anymore without wanting you.*

Heath: *Then maybe we shouldn't be around each other.*

Me: *But I don't know how to do that either.*

Heath: *Then how do we fix this?*

Me: *I think we should avoid being alone. Make sure we're not tempted. Avoid conversations like this one. If we act like friends again, that's what we'll go back to being ... right?*

Heath: *It's worth a try.*

Me: *Okay. I'll see you tomorrow.*

Heath: *One more thing ...*

Me: *Yeah?*

Heath: *Don't wear the blue pants. You have no idea how tempting your ass looks in them.*

Chapter Twenty-One

HEATH

"You're wearing the blue pants." They're the first words out of my mouth Friday morning when I walk in to find Griff standing at the reception desk, booty perfectly cupped and molded in navy cotton. When I drag my eyes away from it, I find Griff is blushing to his ears.

"I was wearing other ones, but then I spilled my tea and —" He checks we're alone. "I swear it wasn't on purpose. They're all I had clean."

"Relax." I'm going to have to get through today with an uncomfortable situation. "It's fine. I was joking anyway." Yeah, I so wasn't. Between those pants and the memory of the side view of his sexy full ass flexing as he fucked me, I'm definitely going to struggle to focus. Which isn't great considering the week we're having. The week where we've been super professional and avoided talking about ... things. Even as the sexual tension crackled around us.

Poppy has stopped dropping by and told us to call her instead if we need anything, so essentially, Griff and I are on our own. And he's ... not taking it well.

He's slower to pick up on the computer work, and it's getting to him. He's quick to get frustrated with himself, gets aggressive with the mouse, and becomes easily flustered on the phone when he's asked a question he doesn't know the answer to.

"Works well under pressure" is not going on Griff's resume.

"Ready to tackle the events calendar?" I ask him.

Griff cringes, which only makes me laugh. "I ... I don't think I can do it. My brain isn't built for this stuff."

"Take a breath." I squeeze his shoulder in support. "There's no hurry to any of this. I'm here. I'm not going anywhere."

"Why not?" he mutters. "Everyone else has."

"Ohh ... sulky Griff has come to work today, has he?"

"Fuck off."

I tilt my head. "Grumpy Griff, then?"

"Better than Shit-stirrer Heath."

"But I *love* Shit-stirrer Heath."

"At least one of us does."

"Naw." I nudge him. "We both know you do too."

That finally gets a small smile.

"Hey ..." I use my sympathy tone. "Don't try to rush

picking it up. It's okay to need some time. You can't be the best at everything."

"The best? At the moment, I can't get anything right."

"Are you forgetting that I've seen the badass chairs you made? And not for nothing, that thing we've agreed we're not talking about, you were easily the best there as well."

"Heath ..." He rubs a hand over his face like he's trying to hide the blush that takes over. "I'm so glad we're not talking about it."

"Me too." And because apparently I have no control when it comes to my mouth, I say, "Since I think about it enough as it is."

Griff leans forward and rests his head on the reception counter. "I can't look at you right now."

"And there you go, getting into position for me."

He jolts upright again.

"Fuck, you're so tense, man," I say.

"I have another whole day of this ahead and then—"

My interest snags on the way he cut off. "And then?"

He sighs and turns panicked eyes on me. "Art's taking me out tomorrow night."

My gut twists so hard I might be sick. "Huh."

"Yeah, I ..." He swallows. "I wasn't planning to say anything, because ... you know."

"Hey, it's fine." I force myself to sound it. "No secrets between us, remember? The sooner we both get over this ... thing ... It's fine. It's *good*."

"Yeah."

And like that, I don't feel like working any more than he does.

We both stare at the computer, not sure what to say to each other. It's not supposed to be like this with Griff.

All I know is that for the first time in my life, I don't want to go out and find someone to have sex with. I don't want something cheap and temporary. And that's kind of terrifying considering the alternative.

"This can wait," I say.

"What?"

"Everything I had planned for today can be done later. Let's take the morning off, let off some steam, and then we can come back later and tackle this with fresh eyes. You need time out to do something fun."

Griff's eyes narrow. "You're not talking about sex, are you?"

I wish I could ignore that slight hope I detect in his voice. "Not at all. But I do have an idea. Grab your stuff."

Griff does what I asked without question. I radio Michelle to man the front desk, and then we swing by Griff's house to get changed. He insists on going inside one at a time to stop anything from happening—which, *come on*, we are grown-ass men and we can't even be in the same room together? It's not like I'd watch him strip off. Unbuttoning his shirt ... peeling those pants down over his thick thighs ... Okay, yep. Our decision to go separately was a good one.

Once we're done, we jump in my car, and I take us to the Killer Brew. The cafe outside is busy, but inside has that quiet hum of a day just starting. Joey is at the bar, and he puts the crate of bottles aside to serve me.

"Two for the axes, thanks."

He rings me up, and then I nod to Griff to follow me.

"Last time you held a sharp object, I ended up injured," Griff points out.

"Just don't try to kiss me and we'll be fine."

The ceiling and floor in here are painted black, and with the dark wood wall behind the targets and the dark wood half walls between each section, the room has a moody, intimate feel, even midmorning.

"I wanted to do this for my birthday last year, remember?"

"I do." Which is why I brought us here. Despite spending so much time at the Killer Brew, I think I've only been in here once before. Griff wanted to hire this whole room for his birthday, but since axes and alcohol don't mix, Poppy convinced him to do it somewhere people could drink instead. "You know, if you'd told her this is what you really wanted, she would have been okay with it."

"I know, but ... it was just easier."

I frown as we retrieve the small axes and set up in our lanes. "You do that a lot, you know?"

"Do what?"

Take the easy route. I want to call him out on it, because the more I think about it, the more I think Griff is used to using his family to hide behind when it comes to hard choices.

His birthday? Poppy won't like it.

The divorce? Felix will be upset.

I'm trying not to ask myself the question, but it floats through my mind anyway. *Is that what he's doing with me?*

I force the thought aside, because today, we're strictly friends. And we're going to goof off and get our friendship back on track. My emotional crisis can take a rain check.

I pick up an axe, line up my target, and toss. It leaves my hand, and I watch as it flips over twice before hitting the target with a *thunk*. The sound calms me, and with every axe, with every throw, the tension bleeds out of me.

When I glance over at Griff, it's clear he feels the same. And it's clear he's a thousand times better at this than me.

"Damn, you got the bullseye?"

"Yeah, what did you ..." He leans over to see around the wire mesh between our lanes and starts to laugh. "Maybe they didn't tell you this, but you're supposed to aim for the middle of the target."

I flip him off. "So I'm not very good at this."

"Like you said, we can't all be the best at everything."

"Hey, there you go proving my point for me."

"Okay, smart-ass."

"But this is where you're supposed to say that at least I'm good at sex."

Griff shifts back to his lane. "You're good at a lot of other things too."

I plant my hands on my hips and wait patiently.

"Including the sex. Happy?"

I want to tell him I'd be happier if we did it again, but I'm being a good friend. "Very."

We take our time, and Joey lets us stay in longer than we paid for since no one else is waiting. After lunch, Griff wants to pick up food from the market that takes up the other side of Killer Brew, so we wander the aisles and pick out ingredients for easy dishes I can teach him to cook.

By the time we drop them at his place, change back into our work clothes, and take over for Michelle so she can have her break, it's one thirty, and Griff looks a thousand times less tense than he did this morning.

"Come on." I lead him into the office, and we keep the door open to make sure we can hear if any guests walk in. "Let's make a list."

"Of?"

"The tasks we're both responsible for. I don't think you're going to be able to get out of all the computer work, but your days are already reasonably full with all you do on the grounds."

I swear I can feel the way he holds his breath. "I think I know enough about the reservations system to handle that."

"Okay, good." I wake up the computer, open a document, and distribute tasks into the two different columns. It doesn't escape my notice that Griff has a lot of the tasks I was responsible for pre-restructure, and I'm taking over a lot of what Poppy did previously. I don't let it get to me. With anyone else, maybe. But not Griff.

And despite him wanting to opt out of anything involving a screen, we spend time running over the events calendar anyway. I show him how to send out confirmations and cross-check that everything is ordered for the correct day it's needed. Halloween week is especially important because the whole week has back-to-back activities and displays.

We're interrupted a few times by guests, and once afternoon hits, we take a walk around the grounds.

Griff makes a show of stretching, and I make a point of not watching him do it. We walk close enough our arms bump, all along the honeysuckle walkways and down the lavender-lined paths. By the time we get back to the reception building, it's after seven, and Michelle is locking up for the day. We have restricted twenty-four-hour service, where there is a handful of us on, working out of the main restaurant and small office there. Safety in numbers and all that.

The second we step inside the dim reception area and close the door behind us, the vibrating energy from earlier is back. The click of the lock is way too loud, and I know what Griff is thinking because it's in my head too.

We should call it a night.

There are a few things left to do that could technically wait until Monday, but I don't like the idea of starting the week behind. But as we head toward the office together and I walk in to find that the small room smells like Griff, I know I need to do something.

I clear my throat. "Want me to finish up here?"

"Nope. I need to learn." He takes a seat at the desk. "You're good at ... *tutorials.*"

Holy fuck.

Chapter Twenty-Two

GRIFF

Where numbers and spreadsheets usually go over my head, this is a thousand times worse. The office has the still energy of a day come to an end, so every movement Heath makes, every word that passes those delicious lips, seems a thousand times more significant than usual.

I can smell him, feel his warmth. Every part of me is yearning to get closer and touch what I can't.

He swallows, loudly, and it's only then I realize he's finished whatever he was saying. I drag my focus away from his lips and meet his warm brown eyes.

"D-did you get that?"

"No." My eyes drop to his lips again. "I missed every word."

"Griff..."

"What?"

"You're supposed to be concentrating."

"I *am* concentrating." I'm concentrating so hard on his lips I can almost feel them on me again. The tingles over my skin. His needy, all-consuming desperation. Blood is pooling in my groin as my body begs for me to close the distance.

"We can't ..." he whispers.

"I know."

"*Griff.*" His voice shakes with want, and it turns me the fuck on. "We *can't.*"

"I *know.*"

That thrumming band inside me snaps, and we move at the same time. Our mouths crash together, Heath's chair flies out from under him, and then he's straddling my lap.

All that agitated need that's been building all week explodes, and the feeling is so addictive, so mind-numbingly golden, I don't know how I'm supposed to survive without it. I clutch him to me, kiss him harder, deeper, wanting nothing more than to stay like this with him forever.

Doubts and cautions try to attack me, but I forcefully push them away. Now we've started, there's no way I can refuse him. Not now. Not Heath.

"Do you need me to stop?" he asks against my lips, hands already working open the buttons on my shirt.

"Don't you dare."

His lips attack under my jaw, forcing my head back as he travels down the column of my throat. "I want you to fuck me again so bad."

"Do you have lube?"

"Shit, no."

Damn. I could run home for some, but I'm scared that if we break this moment, I'll come to my senses, and my conscience will take over. I can't have that. It's not often I let myself indulge, but Heath is apparently my weakness. He's the only one who shuts up that inner voice of responsibility.

"Then this time, I'll take care of you," he growls.

Heath slides off my lap to kneel between my thighs, and the sight of him kissing down my torso has my cock throbbing. It's pressing painfully against my zipper, and as Heath's mouth trails over my stomach, I swear he's getting slower and slower.

"Come on ..." I whine.

The smile he sends me is sinful. "You've made me wait all week." He leans in to drag his tongue over my nipple. "It would serve you right to be teased, considering how much of a tease you are yourself."

"Let's not talk about this week. There's only now. And how you're about to suck my cock."

His eyes darken as he reaches down and undoes his own fly. I watch as he pulls out his hard length and gives it a slow stroke. "Take your cock out."

I hurry to do as he says, but before I can stroke myself, he tells me to stop.

"Hands behind your head. Spread your thighs more."

I do as he says, and once I'm in position, a moan catches in his chest. He strokes himself again, eyes trailing over my body.

"You look like a mess, Griff. A filthy, horny mess, lazing back and waiting for me to touch you."

Oh, dear god.

"You think you deserve my mouth, don't you? Think your cock is a gift to me, that you're being so generous by letting me have it."

Keeping my hands behind my head is becoming impossible. I want to pull him to me, touch him. There's too much distance between us and not enough orgasms. "Please, Heath ..."

"*Make* me."

The force of his words sends shivers through me. I'm still struggling to keep up with what he wants when I reach out and twist my fingers through his short hair. "Like this?"

"Yes ..." He makes a noise in the back of his throat that cuts off before it can form.

I tighten my grip and guide his face lower. "Tell me how much you want this."

"So much. I'll die if I can't have it."

"Stick out your tongue."

He opens his mouth wide, and fuck me, it's a sexy view. I run the tip of my cock gently over his top lip before sliding the underside over his tongue.

"I know I deserve this mouth, but the question is, do you deserve my cock?"

He hurries to nod, stare locked on mine.

"Speak."

"I'll beg if I have to."

I shove into this mouth on a groan, and Heath's lips

immediately wrap around me. I have no clue what this game is, but I do know that the way Heath responds is so fucking hot. My hands rest on his head as he bobs up and down, and only a few seconds in, he about blows my mind. Heath sinks all the way down, and my cock slips into his throat.

"Motherfucker," I gasp, barely able to stand how tight it is.

He swallows around me, and I almost come before Heath pulls off a little and goes back to giving me the blow job of my life. His mouth is so hot, so wet; my hand all these years has been no substitute for the feelings he's awakening in me. Seeing him work me over—but not only that, seeing him *enjoy* it, seeing him *touching* himself over pleasuring me —is rushing to my head and threatening to end this thing far too soon.

My thighs quake with the pressure to keep them from closing around him, and my skin feels too hot. Too tight.

Heath rolls my balls in his palm, and the tingles that are racing from them to my spine to my dick are becoming overwhelming.

I crush his hair between my fingers and coax him faster; then his hand drops from my balls, and one of his fingers slides between my ass cheeks. The second he brushes my hole, I cry out, and my cock finally lets go. I pump into his mouth with each spurt of cum, not stopping until the high recedes.

"You're not making this fair," he complains, climbing back into my lap.

I knock his hand off his shaft and take over, loving the feel of the hard, heated cock in my palm.

"Griff ..." His forehead meets mine, lust-filled brown eyes barely an inch away. I steady him with one hand on his neck while I stroke him like my life depends on it. Every one of his panting breaths hits my mouth, he's clutching the collar of my shirt like I might disappear, and the desperation on his face hits me in the gut because I feel it too.

I don't want this to end here.

I don't want to walk away from this.

I know all the reasons why we shouldn't, but would it be the worst thing in the world to be selfish for once?

"You're thinking again," he says, sounding wrecked.

I force the thoughts away and move my hand from his neck to cup the back of his head. "No, I'm not. I'm here. I'm with you. This is the only place I want to be."

"Kiss me."

I give it to him. Our mouths meet, and even though the kiss is fire, it's not the explosion from earlier. This isn't about sex or chemistry, only that when I'm kissing him, the world makes sense. When I'm kissing him, my heart feels full.

Heath stiffens against me, cum coating my hand and stomach, but we still don't break away from each other. Our kiss slows, lingers, tongues turning lazy after their fight for dominance.

His hands disappear into my hair, and I hold him to me for so long, I lose track of time. It's like neither of us wants to be the one who breaks away first, because I have no idea what comes next.

Risking my relationship with Felix? I can't.

But I'm not so sure I can go on pretending like this meant nothing to me.

Even when our kissing turns to traded pecks and soft caresses, we don't speak. Even when my back protests the position and my thighs feel cramped from where they're crushed together, I don't make a move to get up.

I want to ask him to come home with me. To stay the night and then the one after. But I can't make those kinds of promises yet, and while that was undeniably driven from both sides, while I know he needed that as much as I did, I have no idea where he's at with it all. Opening myself up to that kind of conversation is a risk that comes with a huge side of heartache if it goes wrong.

"So ..." I begin.

Heath straightens. "I know. It can't happen again."

"I want it to."

"Me too." He gives me a wry smile. "But that's a bigger sacrifice on your end than mine."

I almost say I don't care, but that's not true. Choosing sex and knowing it could ruin the relationship I have with my son is so far beyond selfish, it's stupid. I might have been able to overlook that in the heat of the moment, but now my brain is catching up, I'm ... drained.

Especially when I look at Heath and my whole chest feels like it's aching.

I run my hand over my face, and Heath finally climbs off

my lap and tucks himself away. "I'm sorry," I say. "This is a mess."

"It is. But hey, we've got that out of our system now, haven't we?"

"Have we?" I pin him with a dry look. "Is that how we're going to play it?"

"It is, because we're grown-ups and friends and we're going to get through this."

That's not what I want at all though. I stand and fix my clothes before I can force a smile. "Completely out of my system."

"Good. We're agreed. And when you go out with Art tomorrow night, you can have your one-night stand."

My face falls. "Heath, that's the last thing I—"

"No." He covers my mouth. "It's the right thing to do. We never should have started this, because there's no way I can ask you to choose between this and your family. I would never. You need to go out tomorrow night. Whether you hook up or not is completely up to you, but you have to go, and you have to make sure you take me out of the equation."

I don't think that's possible. Hooking up or not, Heath is always in the equation. But if he's set on pretending, I can play along too. "Sure," I say, hating the word. "It's not like Art would let me cancel on him anyway."

Chapter Twenty-Three

HEATH

"I'm telling you, man, you fucked up."

I scowl at Leif because he's not telling me anything I don't already know. "I'm trying to be the bigger person."

"Nope, you're trying to break your heart now so it's over and done with, because you think somehow that will make it easier."

"Are you a therapist now?" I throw back. Before he got together with Barney, Leif and I used to spend a lot of time going out together. He was the year below me at school, but our families go way back, and given we were both forever determined not to settle down, I couldn't ask for a better wingman.

The difference is, he's always been blatantly in love with

his best friend, and Barney could never see it. This thing with Griff is all new.

"We can change the subject if you want, but I know that it doesn't matter what we talk about, you're going to be spending your night thinking about what Griffin is up to."

"You can't know that."

"Can and do. It's why you've dragged me to the gym on a Saturday night. How do you think it was for me when Barney started dating again? I spent most of the nights he was out getting wasted."

"Healthy."

"About as healthy as pretending your feelings don't exist."

He has no idea what he's talking about. "I'm not you. I haven't been pining over Griff since the start of time. We accidentally hooked up, and now things are messy. With a bit of time, we'll be able to put it behind us."

Leif scoffs obnoxiously loud. "No one is buying that, not even you. 'Accidentally hooked up.' How do you accidentally end up with someone's cock inside you?"

"I'm so glad I came to you for advice."

Leif slows down his treadmill so we can talk easier. "Look, when Barney and I were doing the whole friends-with-benefits thing, I might have been too chickenshit to tell him how I felt, but I never tried to fool myself."

"I'm not trying to fool myself, I'm trying to protect myself. And again, it's not the same thing."

"Why? Because I loved Barney forever? What does it

matter if it's years or five minutes? Love is love, dude, and you're going to get hurt no matter how you play it."

I already know all this, which is why the lies and self-deception are necessary. If I can convince myself I'm over Griff, I'll be over him. I won't sit here obsessing about him being out with Art and hooking up with whoever he wants.

I won't focus on the fact that if Griff is the Griff I know, whoever he hooks up with will become permanent, and if it's a man, I'll have to play nice with the asshole when he gets to have what I'm starting to realize I desperately want. All because they've never met Poppy or Felix before.

Which is so fucking ridiculous I might pull my hair out over it. Shouldn't Griff's family be *happy* for him to settle down with someone who's had his back through everything rather than whatever ridiculous rando ends up with their tongue down Griff's throat?

"Well, the growling has me convinced you're totally okay," Leif says.

"New topic."

"Fine. How is the job hunt going?"

And of course he'd change the conversation to the only other subject I don't want to talk about. "It's not."

"What?"

"Griff needs me because Poppy's leaving the resort, so …"

"She's leaving him to run the place? Doesn't she know her ex-husband at all?"

"We both know I'm going to be the one running it."

Leif laughs. "So you're staying. With Griff. Knowing you have feelings for him. And you'll be totally okay to not be able to escape him when he inevitably starts dating again."

"And we're back on Griff."

"How are we supposed to not talk about him when your life literally revolves around him?"

"I have plenty going on that doesn't involve him." Which is true. My family, my friends—Leif, exhibit A—my weekends out. Just because he's a huge part of my life doesn't mean he's all of it.

"I'm only saying that yes, your situation is tough. There was no reason for Barney and me not to be together other than our own idiocy. Griff comes with baggage. I *get* it. But pushing aside what you want all the time because he needs you isn't healthy."

"You're not the first person to say that to me lately."

Leif lifts his eyebrows like *See?* and he can hold the smugness because I get it. "We only say it because we care."

"I know you do. But have you ever stopped and asked yourself if what I want *is* to make Griff happy? Even before the confusing feelings, I loved helping him and being there for him. Why can't that be enough?"

"You sure you haven't been in love with him this whole time?"

I get the feeling we'll face that question a lot. "Platonic love is a very real thing, and it's also all I've ever felt for him."

"Until now."

As much as I want to keep denying it, it's starting to feel ridiculous. "*Fine.* You win. Until now. I don't want to make him happy from the sidelines anymore."

"Then, be selfish."

My laugh is hollow. "And if he loses his family because of me?"

"Then that's their choice. Not yours. Not his. If they put their own comfort over Griff's happiness, then that tells you exactly the type of people they are."

The way he says it sounds so simple, and in theory, I get that it is. But even if Griff and I decide this thing is too important not to take a chance on, if he loses his family because of it, it'll tear him up inside. Losing Felix will kill him, and even with the split, losing Poppy will hurt him as well. Most people would be jealous of how close they are, and while I'm borderline resentful that she's part of the problem standing in my way, I *don't* resent her or her relationship with Griff. They'll always be a part of each other's lives. Whoever he's with next needs to understand that. I do. And if we can make it through this with my own relationship with Poppy intact, I'm going to do it because she's my family too.

It's one of the things that makes being *selfish* so hard. I don't want to hurt any of these people. But then I think of Griff, out with Art, getting hot and sweaty on a dance floor between two dudes like last week, and I know without a doubt that I can't hold back anymore.

I told him to hook up tonight.

There's every chance he has.

And I don't fucking care.

Right now, all that matters is making sure he's never with anyone else again.

Whatever it takes.

Chapter Twenty-Four

GRIFF

I was determined to keep an open mind. Going to a club two weekends in a row feels like overkill, but Art says it's either that or an app. At least with the club, I have the buffer of other people around.

Other people who are all making me very uncomfortable.

I try drinking at the bar with Art, I try dancing, and I even, for one moment, consider taking some guy up on his offer to go out back. I know I'm supposed to, but actually going through with it makes me feel all ... gross.

Not the sex side. Fuck knows I'm always down to have my dick sucked, but ... my heart gives a tug, and the more I look around at the crowded club, the more I know this isn't for me.

Cheap hookups, one-night stands, whatever you want to call them ... Heath was right. I can't do it.

All I keep picturing is sitting on my porch, hands covered in wood dust, a soft kiss hitting the back of my head ... then my best friend taking the spot beside me and filling me in on his day.

I huff out a breath and finish the rest of whatever cocktail Art is making me drink. It's good but powerful. I'm feeling a buzz, but somehow instead of feeling drunker, I'm only getting more sober. And sick.

"The bar doesn't need you to hold it up," Art says, joining me.

"Maybe I need *it* to hold *me* up."

"Either way, that doesn't explain why you turned down the two cuties who hit on you in the last ten minutes."

"Should I be concerned you're more focused on me than the people you're dancing with?" I pretend to gasp. "Are you into me, Art? I hate to say it, but you're not my type."

"No, apparently no one here is. Your type is unavailable best friends, but you've got to move on from that."

"You know what, maybe I don't want to."

Art lifts his dark eyebrows. "So, you're going to tell him how you feel, are you? Let your ex-wife and kid know?"

I clench my jaw against both of those options.

"That's what I thought. Look, I'm not here to push you into anything. I'm here to raise you up and make you shine at whatever goddamn choice you make. Want to get together with Heath? I'll find you a pickup truck you can put a mattress in to bone the night away. Want to tell your ex to go fuck herself? I'll write up the cards. Need your dick sucked by a random? I'll guard the door. But if you want to live in denial and skirt around the truth, then I'm not your guy."

I narrow my eyes. "So what's going on between you and Joey again?"

"Fuck you." Art turns away from me to look back at the dance floor. "Here I am trying to help, and you're bringing that little shit up."

When I was living at home, I spent a lot of time at Killer Brew with Art so I could get out of the house. Art can deny it all he likes—I *know* how he looks at Joey, and while I know that Joey's flirting leads to nothing most of the time, there's something different in the way he looks at Art when Art isn't paying attention.

That guy wants Art's dick. I'd put money on it.

"You said you were all about the honesty," I point out. "Or does that only apply to people who aren't you?"

"Now you're getting it." He winks. Art's ridiculous but refreshing at the same time.

"I think ... I don't think hooking up is for me."

"Yeah, I kind of figured."

"You did?"

He gives me a genuine smile. "Come on. I know you meant it when you said you missed sex, but not everyone is built to go from a long-term monogamous relationship into full-on man-whore mode like me."

"The thing is, I don't think I can view sex as *only sex*. I can't separate the physical from the emotional. It's that deeper connection that I crave, and after having that with

Heath, I can't see me settling for less."

"Well, good for you. I've never had that, so I'm happy to go on making all of my connections with my cock."

I laugh, trying not to picture Art walking around with his dick out, using it to shake people's hands. That image is ... unsettling.

"It's still early. Why don't you come dance with me for a bit, then when I find my trick for tonight, you can take off?"

"Will you touch me inappropriately?" I ask.

"At least a couple of times."

"My D is off-limits though."

"So long as your ass is up for grabs, you've got a deal."

I pretend to think for a moment, then nod. "I accept those terms."

We end up spending more time on the dance floor than I would have pictured, given how shit the night started off. With the pressure to find someone removed, having fun with Art is easy. I forget to worry about being too old or not dressed right. I forget about my frown lines and the fact I have a kid who's almost as old as a lot of the guys here. It's fun.

A bit past midnight, Art points out his target, and as soon as the man is close enough, I switch out places with him. They immediately grind together, and like that, my night is over. Even loosened up and relaxed, my interest in the men here hasn't changed. Because I know, no matter how many people I try to use to get Heath out of my system, none of them could compare.

I wait outside for a cab, and when it finally pulls up, I climb inside, feeling sore and ready for bed. Maybe forty-three isn't too old for this, but *I'm* too old for this. It's not something I enjoy. It's too busy, too loud, and dear god I sound like my dad.

At least I tried it though.

I went out, discovered it's not for me, and now I can cross it off my list and move on. I doubt I'm going to get the guts to tell Heath I want something real with him, but it's time to stop focusing on other people and focus on me. Hookups and relationships aren't the answer to being happy —look at my marriage.

Nope. I need to bring my focus back to what I wanted to achieve when I started this new stage of my life.

I want simple.

I need to do whatever I can to get there.

The business will be a bigger thing to work out, but in about a month, we can tell Felix about the split, so I won't be so anxious about that anymore. Heath ... fuck. I don't know what to do about Heath.

I can't lose my best friend, but I can't even be around him without an ache hitting me so deep and hard that I'll do anything to soothe it. Including throw all responsibility out of the window just to be with him.

He's ... the kind of gorgeous that makes me smile without thought. He's stability. Being around him settles all of me, even if we're not doing anything. I love the moments we joke around and flirt, but sometimes the quiet moments between us are even better.

Maybe those things aren't what people look for in a relationship. Maybe those things are seen as too boring or don't have the exciting edge of the epic romances that sweep people off their feet.

But to me, those things are perfection.

Because they're us.

When we're together, I feel whole.

The cab turns along the drive to the resort, and we make small talk about summer tourists and whether the resort is ready for Halloween. I tell him we are, even though I have no fucking clue, but without Poppy as my safety net, I better get a clue. Half-assing this job isn't going to do anyone favors, least of all my staff.

We round the front, and the driver pulls up in the gravel drive beside the dark reception building.

"You can drop me here."

It's easier than trying to get him to take his car around the back and then out again.

The night is still warm, the scent of flowers heavy on the breeze, and it's lucky I know my way around because it's dark on the path through the trees to my place. The moon isn't very bright tonight, but I can make out enough that I don't go ass over tits.

Apparently I can't make out *that* much though, because when I reach the door, a voice catches me completely by surprise.

"You're home."

I jump for my goddamn life and whirl toward the sound. "I'm armed!"

Instead of sounding threatening though, it comes out like a question, which earns some very familiar laughter.

"*Heath*?"

He steps closer so I can almost make out his features. "Depends what you're armed with."

"A belly full of cocktail I need to piss out and a lifetime's worth of insecurities," I say.

"Interesting."

"What?"

"Well, given how high you jumped, I thought the first problem would have been solved for you."

I'd flip him off if I thought he could actually see it. Instead, I unlock my door. "I haven't wet myself in almost forty years, I'd like to keep my streak alive, thanks."

"Would have been hilarious for me though."

I feel Heath follow me inside and quickly move to flick on the light. As I kick off my shoes, the place floods with sudden brightness, and it takes me a second to focus. I duck into the bathroom to take a leak, and when I step back out, the small, bare room calms my overstimulated nerves.

Until I glance at Heath.

Then the jitters unleash, and I'm left staring at him without knowing what to say.

"So ... good night?" he asks like it's totally normal for him to be waiting at my place at almost one in the morning.

"Yeah, surprisingly." I eye him, and there's something forced about his expression. "What are you doing here?"

"Thought I'd stop by. Offer some emotional support."

He tosses a box of condoms on my coffee table. "Thought I'd bring you a happy hookup gift just in case you forgot..."

"Heath..."

"You could go bare with me since you know I'm not going to lie about my status, but you need to be careful. Dick *or* vagina, STDs are no joke."

"Okay..."

"And maybe I'm too late, or you want to talk about PrEP and we can do that too, but hopefully if you fucked someone tonight, you—"

"I didn't."

"What?" His head shoots up, eyes wider than I've ever seen them. And maybe I'm naive, and maybe I'm clueless about a whole hell of a lot to do with dating, but Heath looks ... relieved?

I step closer. "I didn't hook up with anyone. No sex. No kissing. No touching."

"But ... why?"

I shouldn't answer that. The truth isn't kind to either of us, but it comes out anyway. "Because all I could think about was you."

Chapter Twenty-Five

HEATH

All I could think about was you.

With those magic words, I almost throw myself at him. Sure, he could have meant it in a bad way or the comparisons or ... whatever. But I can read him. His face, his tone, his words.

He's mine as much as I'm his.

Nothing has changed though. Just because we both want this doesn't mean we're ready to throw everything else away.

He sighs, blue eyes flicking away toward the chairs he made. They're sitting by the door, waiting for a table, and Griff paces toward them and drops down onto one. He looks like a kid in the naughty corner.

On one hand, he's definitely being too hard on himself.

On the other, I get it. Poppy is a total unknown in how she'd react. She's levelheaded and logical, and there's every chance she won't feel completely betrayed, but when I flip perspectives and try to imagine her and Griff telling me they're seeing each other after years of it being the three of us, I'd be hurt—*no*. I'd be furious. I'd assume the worst of the both of them.

Here's to hoping she's a better human than me.

Felix, on the other hand ... he rides high on his emotions. The divorce will be hard enough without finding out his father is seeing a man and that man happens to be his pseudo-uncle.

I hang my head back on a groan. "I'm sorry. I shouldn't have come here." I needed to though. I came because I couldn't sleep—I couldn't stop picturing Griff in bed with someone else.

"I thought you were bringing me a *getting back out there* gift?" he says around a wry smile.

"Happy hookup. They're totally different things. And since you didn't hook up, I guess I'll have to take them with—"

"Heath." He pats the chair beside him. "Sit down."

I take a deep breath, then do as he says. We're quiet for a moment before I whisper, "Nothing has changed. I can't ask you to risk giving them up."

"Yes, but I refuse to give you up either." He reaches out to tilt my face toward him. "And you're not asking. The way I see it, I have two options. I deny how I'm feeling and try to put distance between us, knowing that I'd be hurting us both—"

"I'd do it if you need me to."

"I know. You'd do anything for me."

"I would." I swallow. "Gladly."

"Then tell me this. With everything else taken out of the equation, would you want a relationship with me?"

My heart answers for me. The ache is so intense and insistent that I can only say one thing. "Yes."

"Then that brings me to my other option."

"Which is ..."

Griff's brow pulls down briefly. "I'm scared," he says. "For both of us. As far as anyone knows, Poppy and I have been apart for a few weeks, as opposed to the year it's been. You don't deserve the type of gossip that comes from a suspected affair, and I can't tell the truth and clarify things if it means getting back to Felix that we lied to him."

"You know I don't care about what people think."

"You don't, but I do. It's not only that though. The thing I'm most scared about is what happens if we don't work out? What if we try this and then I end up losing my family *and* you?"

"Honestly, Griff, I don't see us being able to go back to how we were."

"I know what you mean."

Silence takes over us again, both of us trying to see a way out of this. No one knows we've hooked up, so it's not too late to end this, but ... "Wait. No one knows about us."

"Well ... Art does."

I'm not surprised he told him. "Leif too, but that's only because we told them. No one else knows."

"How could they?"

"Exactly. It's not like we have sex in front of people, and as friends, we're together most of the time. No one would know."

"You want to be together in secret?"

"Not long term," I clarify. "But I understand you not wanting to tell anyone until you're more sure about this. It's a huge change for us. I get it. I don't want to be your secret forever, but while we work out things and figure out where we stand, why not?"

"Why not?" Griff mutters.

Even though this has to be his choice, I can't help but give him my whole truth. "I can't walk away from you."

"So don't." He stands and pulls me to my feet. His warm arms wrap around me, and I press closer to him like he's the only thing keeping me standing. "Let's do it."

"Yeah?"

His lips brush over mine. "I can't walk away from you either."

"Then take me to bed."

Griff locks up, then takes my hand and leads me through to the bedroom. We pause by the bed, mouths finding each other in a kiss that makes my toes curl. It's hard but unhurried, our tongues exploring each other's mouths as though it's the first time, and the way he holds my face and controls the kiss has flutters bursting in my gut.

I break the kiss as I unbutton his shirt, and my lips find

every inch of skin as it's exposed. I work down his body until I'm kneeling at his feet, and then I help him out of his shorts and boxer briefs.

Griff's hard cock is mouthwatering, and no matter how I teased him about not measuring up, it was all bullshit because it's quickly becoming my favorite sight. Instead of giving in to my urges and swallowing him down, I stand again and nudge Griff so he falls back on the bed. His bedroom light is off, but the one still on in the living area gives us enough of a glow to see by. The darkness creates interesting shadows across his body. I could jerk myself off to the view and die happy, but tonight, I want his ass.

I remove my clothes as I drink in Griff lazily stroking himself. The way the tip of his cock reappears and disappears inside his foreskin shouldn't be so fucking hot, but I can't drag my eyes away.

When I'm finally naked, I climb up over the top of him.

"I want inside you," I tell him, wondering if it's going to be too much too soon.

With one hand on the small of my back, he rocks his cock up against mine. "It's like you read my mind."

As desperate as I am to get inside of him, I take my time. We kiss for what could be hours, loving the luxury of not needing to hurry. The last two times, the sex has been needy and intense, but that knowledge that we shouldn't be doing what we were doing hung heavy at the back of my mind. Our agreement to keep things between us for now has filled me with freedom to explore these feelings that I never wanted to have.

I don't feel bad admitting that, because Griff knows that I've never wanted love. Never wanted to date with the hopes of finding someone to spend forever with because I was perfectly happy alone. I was fulfilled.

But ... but maybe I felt that way because I already had my person to spend the rest of my life with. The person I already loved with everything I had. The sex didn't reveal these feelings, simply took what I already had and tweaked it. Tailored it. Adjusted our love to this new stage in our relationship, and now that I've felt this high, I never want to go back.

My skin is raw from kissing by the time I go for the lube. Griff's heavy stare is on me, watching me pump a healthy amount onto my fingers.

"Have you had anything up there before?" I ask.

He nods. "My fingers when I jerk off."

"Mm. You're going to have to show me that one day."

"One day?" He snorts. "We can do that next. But I want to see you do it right after."

A laugh falls from my mouth. "I'm going to have to work to keep you satisfied, aren't I?"

"You act like you're not every bit as horny as me."

When it comes to Griff, that's one hundred percent true. Keeping my hands off him is torture. "Spread your legs."

He bends his knees and plants his feet on the mattress, letting his legs fall open. He clears his throat. "I'm not sure ... the whole manscaping thing. I don't know how far I need to take it."

I dip my fingers into his crease and meet his eye. "All of you is perfect. Hair, no hair. None of it matters but you."

"Damn, Heath." His voice cracks. "The way you're looking at me is going to go to my head."

"Good." I press my finger against his hole and slowly work it open. "I don't ever want you to doubt how special you are."

"*Nrgh*, I need you."

I work him open, stretching and rubbing until he's relaxed against my fingers. Every time his cock flags, I treat it to a few strokes before turning my attention back to his ass. I'm purposely avoiding his prostate, clearly frustrating him, but I need him to last long enough for me to push inside.

"You look so sexy," I say. "Waiting for me to fuck you into oblivion."

He trembles.

"My fingers aren't enough, are they? You want my fat cock splitting you open."

"Yes ..."

"Tell me."

"I'm desperate for you to fill me."

Griff might joke about being horny all the time, but there's nothing sexier than seeing how much he wants me.

I free my fingers and pump the lube onto my cock this time before rubbing it over my shaft. Griff is focused on the movement, making everything feel heightened, more intense.

"You okay?"

He nods. "I need this."

"Me too." I press one of his thighs up toward his chest, then get myself into position. He's working on his breathing, steadying it, and when he's about to let out another long exhale, I press my cock against his hole and push forward. His breath catches, and I pause, giving his thigh a reassuring squeeze. "Keep breathing. Yeah ... like that."

His hands are fisting the sheets, and his cock is softening as I continue to work myself inside, but he doesn't once ask me to stop.

When I bottom out, I tug him into a kiss, waiting and hoping for him to get more comfortable.

"This still good?" I murmur against his lips. Every part of his body is pressed against mine.

"You have no idea." He squirms beneath me. "Move."

I start out slow with long, controlled thrusts as I give all my attention to his mouth and neck. My free hand roams over his body, running through the hairs on his chest, feeling the way his skin prickles with goose bumps and his nipples pull into hard peaks.

Griff's steady breathing has gone off-balance as he clutches me tighter with every thrust. His eyes are piercing even in the darkness, and it hits me with total clarity how much I need him.

A groan rumbles deep in his chest as he tilts his head back, stubble scraping my nose, to give me access to the place under his jaw that drives him fucking crazy.

Then before I know what's happening, he grabs me and

flips us. I slip out of his ass for a second before he sits up to straddle my waist and sinks back onto my cock.

"Griff?"

"I'm so close." His cock, which was unsure before, is back in the game, standing straight and tall toward the ceiling. He starts to bounce on my cock, taking himself in hand, and just when I thought he couldn't look any sexier, he goes and proves me wrong. Seeing his large, strong body above me while he drives himself toward orgasm pushes me that much closer to the edge.

I hold his waist and pound up into him, making Griff cry out as I peg his prostate over and over. He's panting, and the bead of precum at his slit is growing and taunting me for a taste.

His hand cups my jaw and angles my face back up until I meet his eyes. He's struggling to hold on. Struggling not to give in, but with each passing second, his frown deepens and his eyes grow heavier, and I can tell he's struggling to keep eye contact.

So am I.

I'm fucking him so hard and fast my stomach muscles are cramping up. Griff's thighs are quaking, his body twitching. And I try so desperately to hold out for him ... a bit ... longer.

His strangled gasp and the cum hitting his chest are all I need to let go. I pump into him with each pulse of my cock, his ass milking out my release, and the pleasure is so perfect, a smile slips over my face.

Sex has never been like this. Fulfilling me in every way I

never knew I needed. Just the two of us, owning each other, blindingly in sync.

Griff lets out a breathy laugh. *Yeah,* his eyes say. *That was really something.*

It was, I agree. *And I'm going to protect that something with my life.*

Chapter Twenty-Six

GRIFF

The rules for staying platonic are well and truly out the window.

Everything is goddamn perfect. Heath and I fall into our relationship like it's the way we've always been. There's no awkwardness, no disagreements, just hanging out with my best friend, with the additional benefit of sex at night.

I'm refusing to think about how Felix and Poppy will react because that's something future Griff can deal with.

Heath helps out—badly—with building my dining table, and while it would be faster and easier if he didn't, I enjoy spending the time creating something together.

Work is …

I pause in my carving to look out over the courtyard. Heath went into the office early because he had something to work on, leaving more handpicked flowers on the counter. Every time I see them, I get this patter in my chest. It's not the flowers themselves; it's that Heath knows me so well. He knows that nature has always had a calming effect.

I wish I could help him the way he helps me, but where Heath made it harder while we were building the table, I make everything harder the second I'm in front of the computer.

He told me in the nicest way possible that it takes less time when he's not having to fix all of my mistakes, which made me feel ... worthless. Incapable.

It wasn't his fault, and I know he didn't want to make it sound that way, but I've always thought of myself as a competent person. I'm good with my hands. I pick up practical things easily—after only a few weeks, Heath has me cooking like a pro—but when it comes to running this place, it's a lot more than making sure the rooms are ready and the place looks good. The computer work is slow and tedious, and it makes me drift off, but it's not even that. It's the *lists* and the *tasks* and the fact I always need to be thinking ahead and have a contingency plan for everything. My brain doesn't work like that.

My thought process is linear, one task at a time. I need a table and chairs? I go out, I find the wood, I make it.

Heath practically has fucking flow charts for what to do in all of the worst-case scenarios. The resort floods? He's got it covered. Overbooked? He has a work-around. Shitty service? He has a seven-point system for saving face with the guests and retraining our staff while keeping calm and offering his customer-ready smile.

The other day, someone asked me why we don't offer fluffy robes in the cabins, and my brain barely worked fast enough to splutter out, "I dunno, *should* we?" while I sweated under the scrutiny.

I'm letting Heath down.

I look down at the wooden flower I'm carving. It's a gift for Heath, like he requested, and it's taking longer than usual because I only work on it when he's not around. But does a hunk of wood really make up for all the extra stress I'm putting on him?

There's one idea I've had circulating for the last week or so—I could sell the resort. It would go for a good amount too. I could find somewhere quiet to live, focus on making furniture for a living, put all this stress behind me ... but when I think of walking away from the place I practically built with my bare hands, the ache goes deep. Maybe I struggle with the mechanics of the business side, but I've put everything into this place. I've given the better part of my life to it, and the thought of walking away from something I've had for almost as long as my son drives home the anxiety of everything changing.

My phone starts ringing inside, so I dust myself off and go to answer it. Surprisingly, it's Heath.

"Hey, what are you—"

"We have a problem." And by the way his normally calm tone is strained, this isn't a small problem.

"You need me?"

"Right now. Please."

I hang up, change my shirt into one that doesn't stink like sleep sweat, and jog to the office. The not knowing what's up has a million wild thoughts racing through my mind, and before I can get to the office, the large crowd of people down by one of the end rooms makes the back of my neck prickle.

"What is it?" I demand as soon as I step into reception. Heath hurries over to steer me away from the guests at the counter who look close to tears.

"A pipe burst in room eleven," he says. "Water is coming through the roof and vents ... I'm worried the ceiling is going to collapse. I-I don't know what to do ..."

"Water and electricity off yet?"

"No, I—"

I nod and disappear back out the way I came, rounding the side of the building to the fuse box. I cut off the power to the whole building, then go to the main water valve and turn that fucker off too. The entire resort is about to be out of operation, and we're going to have complaints coming out of our ears, but it's not like we have a choice here.

With that taken care of, I head for room eleven, sidestepping the small crowd outside of it, and stroll inside.

Holy shit. There's a definite bow in the ceiling, with a large wet patch steadily leaking water. The light fixtures and air-conditioning vents are dripping too.

This is going to be a big job.

"What's the damage?" Heath asks, following me inside.

"Yeah, this room is going to be out for a while."

"Hours or ..."

"A couple of days, at least."

He swears under his breath.

"Fully booked?" I ask.

"Yep. Think you can fix this, or should I call a plumber?"

I shrug. "I won't know until I get up there and check the damage, but hold off calling until I can have a look."

"All right. While you do that, I'm going to have to notify everyone that we're out of power and water for the day, which won't be fun, and then see what I can work out for these guests." His gaze slides to where an open suitcase is soaked. "We're going to have damages to pay for ... accommodation to book ..."

"I doubt there's anywhere free in town."

"We might get lucky." By his cringe, I can tell he doesn't believe that.

"No chance they live close enough to cut their trip short?" I ask.

"They only arrived yesterday, and it was a four-hour drive."

Yeah, turning back around isn't ideal.

I huff and run a hand over my face. Who do we know that has somewhere suitable? Heath mentioned how he tried to find free rooms a month or so ago, and I can't see that's changed considering we're about to hit October. I need somewhere available, with decent land, quiet ...

I might actually know a place. "You deal with getting the message out, and let me make a call. I might have an idea."

"Fuck, I hope so, because I'm all out." He glances

behind us before dropping a quick kiss on my cheek and leaving. My one bright spot on this shitty day.

I turn back to the bowed ceiling, readying myself for a long day ahead. There's no way to know how long the pipe was leaking for or the kind of damage I'm going to find when I open up the ceiling. My fingers are crossed that I can fix it myself, and in the meantime, I need a solution for these guests.

I pull out my phone and call Payne, feeling bad for even needing to ask this, but all of my hopes are literally on his shoulders.

He answers after only a few rings.

"What's up?"

"I'm really sorry, but I need a favor."

He hums. "I'm listening."

"Any chance you've fixed up that cottage you bought?" A few months ago, Payne bought a huge plot of land that came with a cute old cottage and ponds on the grounds. It's ten minutes from here, so while it's not a perfect solution, it's all we have.

"Yeah, for the most part. There are still a few things I want to do, but they can be worked out once I've moved in."

"So you haven't moved in yet?"

"No ..." His tone is cautious, and I don't blame him.

"Here's the thing ..." I explain what's happened before launching into my favor. "We *really* need somewhere for these people to stay. I'll pay you their nightly rate if they go for it, obviously."

He's quiet, and I hope he's thinking through logistics

rather than how to say no. "I was planning to start moving in this weekend, but I'd be lying if I said Beau wouldn't be happy about me staying here a couple more days."

I still have no idea why he's bothering to move out at all, considering they're dating, but I figure that's their business. "You'd be saving my ass," I say, not above begging. If this is my chance to help make something easier on Heath, I'll take it.

"One condition," he says.

"Anything."

"Stop hitting on Beau, joking or otherwise."

Despite the stress I'm under, I crack up laughing. Okay, maybe I take it a little far in the group texts, but it took forever for Payne to figure out he had feelings for the guy. "You want to ruin my fun like that?"

"Those are my terms, take it or leave it."

"Deal." I could point out it's an easy deal to make considering no one could measure up to Heath, but I keep that to myself. The fewer people who know, the better.

"Okay, then. You can pick up the keys, and the place is yours. I've already bought a couch and bed that are set up there, but there are no utensils, coffee maker, TV ... it's still pretty bare."

"I'll sort it out."

We say goodbye, and I heave a massive sigh of relief as I end the call and text Heath the details, then get to work.

There's too much water in the roof cavity to see what I'm dealing with, so I clear out the room, then have to wait for the water to drain out of the holes I've drilled in the ceiling. After that, I get up and have another look, and when I'm confident I can handle it myself, I roll up my sleeves and get on with it.

Being covered in filth and water, cutting away a section of the ceiling to see what we're dealing with, carting soggy wet plasterboard out of the room ... it's frustrating that this happened at all, but there's nothing like the satisfaction of fixing something. Of feeling capable again.

I work as fast as I can, conscious that we need the power and water back on. We're lucky this happened during the day while most of our guests are out, because if it was the afternoon and we couldn't run the restaurant, people would be pissed. Thankfully, the buffet breakfast was ready long before now, and we have cafe options for lunch.

The rest I'm confident Heath can handle, because I swear that man can take on anything.

And for the first time since Poppy left, I'm confident I'll be able to handle this too.

Chapter Twenty-Seven

HEATH

A to-do list is racing through my mind so fast I'm struggling to make sense of it. Normally I thrive under pressure, but it's not often I have this many things coming at me at once.

All right, slow it down, Heath.

Griff has got *something* organized for accommodation, so that's my most pressing issue taken care of—if Payne's cottage works out.

First, I need to cover my usual work here so I can deal with the mess, and thankfully, Jody agrees to come in for an extra shift. We have day passes for a horse-riding stable that I give the guests from room eleven—along with reassurances we'll handle everything—and with them out of the way, my brain finally has room to process.

Normally everything I do needs to be run past Poppy, so

the freedom to make a call without having to explain myself is intimidating. I'm not sure if I'm making the right choices here, but her guidance won't be around forever. I have to back myself.

First up, letting all the staff know what's happening, along with the guests who are still on-site. Those in the cabins farther out should be fine as they work off a separate power supply than the main building, but I have no idea how the water works.

As if on cue, the reception phone rings, and from the sounds of Jody's conversation, the complaints are already starting.

Okay ... if there's anything I've learned since working here, it's that people like to feel heard. Usually their complaints are over minor inconveniences that only require an apology, but this is a bit more than minor, and my solution needs to reflect that we understand the issue and are terribly sorry it occurred.

Yeah, because we really asked for the stupid pipe to burst.

Urg. This is the part of customer service that I hate.

I shake the bitterness away, but I can't stop my thoughts from drifting toward the job I interviewed for. Staff training. That was it. No management, no guests, only dealing with the employees and making sure they're taught the highest standards.

If something like this happened, it wouldn't be my problem. That idea is way too tempting. Just saying *fuck it all* and walking out. It would serve Poppy right for leaving Griff to do this alone. She knew he wasn't ready.

But walking away would mean leaving Griff, and that's not something I can do. The last few weeks together have been ... magic. Sure, obviously the sex is great, but the thing that makes everything so different is the deep feelings I have for him. I love him. In a way I never believed I'd be able to love anyone, because when I look at Griff, I see those years behind us, as well as every single year we have ahead.

I leave the office and head for my car, shaking thoughts of Griff away. There's no point thinking of the future or the past when the present is a shitshow.

Griff's text has information on where to pick up the keys from, the address of the property for our guests to stay, and a list of items we might need to source.

Given the vague details there, I decide to grab the keys and drive out to the house myself.

When I arrive, I'm pleasantly surprised. It's small and quaint, but the location is a dream. Inside carries the rustic look throughout with a timber kitchen and hardwood floors, and despite the lack of amenities, this is as good of an option as any. I walk around, writing a list for myself of what I need to pick up, and then I jump back in the car and call Poppy.

"Good morning," she says, sounding way too chipper when we currently have an emergency on our hands.

"Hey, it's me."

"I know," she says. "Everything okay?"

"Truth or a lie?" I ask.

She takes a moment. "How bad?"

"Burst pipe over one of the rooms. Griff is trying to fix it now, but we've got water and power off to most of the site and displaced guests we need to find a home for."

Poppy swears under her breath. "I have to say, I'll take a random accident over you two knuckleheads screwing up any day."

I grit my teeth, because I've had to call her twice this week to reverse a mistake Griff's made in our accounting software. "We're doing the best we can given you up and left with next to no notice."

"That's not fair."

"Isn't it?" And I definitely shouldn't be picking a fight with not only my boss, but the ex-wife of the man I'm in love with, but this needs to be said. "You gave us hardly more than a week to train Griff and get used to you not being here."

"Yes, but I knew he'd have you. I wasn't worried."

"And did it even occur to you to ask?"

"W-what?" She sounds genuinely confused, which softens me toward her.

"You're the one who said I always do whatever Griff wants me to, but you also didn't bother to check in with me that I'd be okay basically taking on the place. You knew Griff would never be able to do what you can. You set him up to fail. And without me, he would have. But instead of assuming I was happy to step up, you should have asked. You should have checked I was okay with taking on that much extra responsibility because from where I stand, I'm doing the work of an owner, not a guest liaison, which isn't fair on me."

"Heath, I'm ..."

"Look, it's fine. Because you're right. I will do anything for Griff, but that's because it's what I choose to do. I don't like having that choice taken away."

"You're right," Poppy says. "I'm sorry."

"Thank you." Damn that feels good to get off my chest. And maybe I'm pushing my luck, but I follow it up with, "I'm on my way to pick up your card for the business account."

"Do I want to know?"

"Nope. These two knuckleheads have got it handled."

"Okay ... I'll run it out to your car."

She's true to her word when ten minutes later, I pull up out the front of the place she used to share with Griff. A flood of memories comes back, of birthdays and Christmases, of Super Bowl Sundays, and late afternoons in summer where Griff and I would sit out the back and watch Felix play as a kid.

This was their life, but it was also mine. I'm struggling to separate the two.

Poppy hurries down the front path, and I try to draw up some kind of bitterness at her. Some annoyance that she's the reason Griff and I aren't public, that she got to have him for as long as she wanted, that she's turned around and dumped too much responsibility in his lap, but ... I can't.

It's easy to try and blame everything on her in theory, but when we come face-to-face, I see my friend who I've shared countless lunches with, who took the time and energy to walk me through how the business works, who I helped build Magnolia Ridge from the ground up. Not physically like Griff did, but the culture, the brand, the type of service that makes people want to visit.

"Hey ..." I say before she can run off again. "Thanks for not questioning me on this."

"I trust your judgment." She shrugs. "Just don't fuck it up."

And even though I know she means today, I can't help reading into it more by telling myself she doesn't want me to fuck up her trust.

Well, too late for that.

I fucked up her trust the second I shoved my tongue down Griff's throat.

The funk doesn't leave me the whole time I'm out buying things for Payne's cabin. Bedding, cushions, styling pieces, and rugs that Griff can use in his place once these guests have gone, a coffee machine that will end up in the office, and a huge flat-screen that could end up in reception with footage of all the best things Kilborough has to offer. Spending this kind of money isn't ideal, but I keep telling myself it's better than a disastrous review and can all be written off.

Plus, I told Griff I was planning on making his place more homely; I just happen to be using his money to do it.

After a day of running around, getting the resort back operational, and putting gift baskets together, I drop the final one off along with an apology. Overall, our guests were understanding, but it helps that most were out for the day.

Even without any dramatic confrontations, I'm drained.

I want to clock out and find Griff. To hold him and breathe in his scent. To relax in his arms. Unfortunately, the couple from room eleven aren't back yet, and when they finally return, tired and wary about the state of their belongings, it takes some serious car salesman talking to get them to agree to their new accommodation.

I ask them to leave any clothes they need a dry cleaner for with reception, then write up a list of damaged items for me to go over. We pay for their car there and give them the number for reception so they can call in the morning when they're ready for us to drop off breakfast.

And by *us*, I mean me.

"You look beat," Jody says when they're finally gone.

"That was ... intense." I groan, thinking of all the work I have waiting. I got here early to take care of it, and that ended up being a complete failure.

"Nope, not happening." Jody plants her hands on her hips. "Don't even think about going back there."

"But—"

"No. Home. Now. The rest will wait."

Yeah, for me. But I'm too tired to argue with her. "You're like a snappy little Chihuahua," I mutter.

"My heart. It bleeds."

I snigger at her deadpan expression, then grab my things and get out of there. Room eleven has been left open with fans running to dry it out, but Griff isn't there.

Instead of going home, I go straight to his place and find him sitting outside waiting for me.

He's still filthy, but I don't hesitate to step into his arms when he opens them.

"You okay?" he asks.

"Tired. You?"

"Sore." Griff chuckles, and the warm sound by my ear goes a long way toward making me feel better. His lips meet mine briefly before I pull back to eye him.

"You're in a good mood."

"Well, yeah." He gives me a bashful look. "I'm kinda proud of us."

"You are?"

"Of course. That was an epic fuckup, but between the two of us, we fixed it."

Huh. I hadn't thought about it that way. But ... he's right. I organized logistics; he solved the accommodation problem and all of the repairs. We played into our strengths, and it was hard, but it worked.

I let out the first real smile I've worn all day. "We did, didn't we?"

"Yep. Now come on. I've been waiting all day to shower, and you're coming in with me."

Chapter Twenty-Eight

GRIFF

Heath needs to bring some clothes over. The number of times he's stayed with me this week and had to leave early so he could go home to grab work clothes is getting ridiculous. Is it too soon to suggest clearing a drawer out for him? It doesn't feel soon.

I shift his sleeping form over and wriggle my arm out from under him. The last thing I want to do is get out of bed, but even though I spent the day working my ass off, I can't sleep. Heath is stressed. It weighed on him all night, and I want to do something to help.

Before the pipe explosion, he said he was going into the office to reply to a few emails and fix up the account queries he had.

Those should be things I can do. And since I can't sleep anyway, I might as well try to work through most of them so when Heath wakes up, he won't have to rush off because it will be taken care of.

Maybe I can even *take care* of *him* before he leaves.

I make my way around to reception, let myself inside, and disable the alarm. Since this building is separate to the rest of the resort, we run our after-hours service through the restaurant so there's more than one person there.

All the information Poppy and Heath have run me through over the past few weeks is written in a notebook in the office desk, so I figure by following it to the letter and not trying to remember any of it, I'll easily be able to manage this.

The emails are straightforward things that even I can handle. Website enquiries and date confirmations are a cinch.

The accounts though ...

I open the software and stare blankly at the screen for a full minute before what I'm looking at makes any kind of sense. No matter how many times I refer back to my notes, I'm still so confused. Maybe I missed steps while writing them down, but it all reads like gibberish to me, and I've got no clue where to start.

Last time I tried to do this, I somehow ended up paying someone twice. Heath didn't even know that was possible, so yay me for exceeding expectations, I guess?

My eyes go unfocused as I try to work out whether to move forward with this or not. On the one hand, I want to impress Heath. I want him to wake up happy and destressed, knowing that I can handle this. On the other hand, I'll do the complete opposite if I fuck up again.

I run a hand over my face in frustration. If I was even a tiny bit more confident than I am now, I wouldn't hesitate to get the job done. Hell, put me in front of a huge pine that needs to be brought down and I wouldn't break a sweat over the thought, but numbers on a screen?

I cringe and look down at my phone. There *is* one person who can help me. It's almost midnight, but Poppy has always been a late sleeper and an early riser. I'm sure she wouldn't have a problem walking me through it.

I'd have to tell her why I'm up though. And why Heath didn't deal with the accounts today or even tomorrow morning. That conversation is dangerous because it could lead to the uncomfortable declaration that I've been holding his tense body for the past few hours and I want to take that tension away. Plus ... with how happy I am that Heath and I pulled off this save together today, calling Poppy doesn't sit right.

It's almost like it cheapens our victory.

It's not as though I have a huge number of options though. I either call her and prove I have no idea what I'm doing, or possibly fuck up and cause Heath more stress, *or* leave it for him to do on top of the rest of his work tomorrow.

It's official: Poppy leaving screwed us.

There's a tiny nudge in the back of my mind that makes that thought feel like a lie. It's not though ... is it? Her leaving has put us in a mad scramble for how to restructure the place, but ... I glance back at the screen. Having all this responsibility land with the one person probably wasn't smart or sustainable to begin with.

Yes, we believed we'd always be together, and the resort's important to us. Her running this place until we died should have been a given, but neither of us took into account what happens in the event of an accident. Sure, Heath knows most of what she did, but with her gone, Heath can't take so much as a sick day without falling behind. I'd thought if I could learn it, that would help, but the more I try, the less information sticks with me, so it's probably time to face that I'm not the solution either.

We need someone else.

Or multiple someones, more likely.

Then I do something I rarely do: I pull out some paper and write a list. I strain my memory for every single task that needs to be done on a daily basis, then start splitting them up within their roles. Seeing it all laid out like that ... yeah, Heath does *a lot* more than any other guest liaison. Do we have enough money to restructure some of the roles? We've been turning a good profit, even with Poppy still taking her share, so I'm confident we could find the money somewhere.

And at this point, it's less of a *maybe* and more something that we have to make happen.

"What are you doing?"

The soft voice from the doorway almost makes me piss myself.

"*Heath.* Do you get off over scaring the shit out of me?"

He laughs softly, joining me in the room. "It's fun to see you jump like that."

"Wow. If I'd known terror turned you on, I would have attached a car battery to my crown jewels when you fucked me."

"And while I appreciate the lengths you'll go to in order to turn me on, I think we can both pass on that idea."

I give him a small, indulgent smile. "Why are you awake?"

"Dunno." Heath perches on the side of the desk. "But when I rolled over and reached for you, you weren't there." His thumb brushes my cheek. "So why are *you* awake?"

I eye him to see if I can pick up on any of the stress that was sitting heavily over him earlier, but all I see is my usually relaxed best friend. With a sigh, I sit back in the desk chair and decide on the truth. "I wanted to help out. Or try to. I hate seeing you stressed, and I especially hate when I'm the cause of some of that."

"You're not—"

"I am though. And I'm sorry. I really am, but I don't get this stuff. I've tried, and it's not getting any easier."

"That's okay though, because we've split the jobs we're doing. I don't expect you to deal with the accounts any more than you expected me to deal with that pipe. We have our strengths."

"Thank you."

"For?"

"Never making me feel like an idiot."

"How would I even manage that when you're one of the smartest guys I know?"

"Smart?" I'm not even being modest when I say I'm not *that*.

"Smarts aren't all about rocket science." Heath presses his hand to the center of my chest. "You're smart where it counts. You're practical, you know what's important, you always think of others before yourself. And that's what makes it so easy for me to put you first. Because no one else does. Not even you."

"Heath ..." How did I get so lucky to share my life with him? First as my best friend and now as that and so much more.

He slides onto my lap. "Now will you leave this and come back to bed?"

"Yes, but ... I think we need to talk about everything you've taken on for me here. I know you said it's okay and you're happy to put me first, but that shouldn't also mean putting you last. So tomorrow, I want to come up with a plan to start distributing some of the other things you do that you should hand off."

"Like ..."

Like everything I should have reorganized already. "Like checking that guest rooms are done and confirming reservations. Those are all things that the guest relations liaison should do. I ... we both know you're the one running this place. I think you need a new title. Maybe ... management?"

I can tell he wants to argue, but after thinking for a minute, he nods.

"Okay. If that's what we need to do."

"Yeah?"

"Yeah … Just wondering whether I should order a new name tag. *Manager in charge* sounds good, but *The Boss* is authoritative and to the point. Imagine how many guests I could pick up with all of that BDE."

I crack up laughing and dig my fingers into Heath's ribs as he tries to plead mercy.

Thank fuck he agrees. If I'm going to get that ultimate relaxed life that I want, it includes my partner sharing it with me. There's no way Heath can enjoy a simple life with too many responsibilities hanging over his head.

And even though I didn't get everything done that I wanted, I let him drag me back to bed, knowing with that plan, things will start to get easier.

Chapter Twenty-Nine

HEATH

Griff's plan for a restructure has added extra pep in my step. Even with the mounting workload, I can see hope at the end of a long, long tunnel.

After dropping breakfast off to our misplaced guests, I lock myself away in the office, determined to get through my to-do list. The emails Griff sent were perfect, but I'm thankful he didn't touch the accounts, and even though I make good time on everything, I'm still behind.

He's right.

I can't keep doing all this myself.

But I was also right in that he can't be the one to help me. Pushing Griff to learn and do these things he doesn't understand or enjoy will never be the answer. If they tried to put me in charge of maintenance of the place, I'd walk out on the spot.

It's not my specialty, and office work isn't his.

We balance each other.

That thought is way more welcome than the others trying to sabotage my good day.

Like the phone call Griff had with Felix this morning. He's still having to play happy families.

Him pretending to still be with Poppy doesn't annoy me, because I know that part of their relationship is over, and I'm not self-conscious about her—Griff would never give me a reason to be.

The thing weighing on me is knowing how much it hurts Griff to lie.

It was there this morning in his slumped form and fake-happy voice as he talked to Fe about coursework and said Poppy had gone to meet up with friends.

Before Felix left for college, Griff retreated into himself and more or less hid out from the world. I've been thrilled with the way he's slowly opening up again since the split. I'd missed that man.

When the workday ends, I've barely seen my man he's been so busy with jobs around the place on top of fixing up room eleven, so when he tells me he's pulling a late one, I give him a sneaky kiss goodbye and drive out to see Mom. I haven't been doing that anywhere near as much as I'd like.

The whole way there, I keep my window down, letting the cool breeze fill the car and ruffle my hair. It's getting dark earlier now, and once we hit winter, this drive is going to be a pain in the ass. I hate driving in the snow, especially on some of the quieter roads out of Kilborough.

I pull into her drive, my cheeks stinging from the wind, and find Mom sitting on her front porch.

I'm stiff as I climb out of the car and approach.

"What are you doing out here?" I ask when I'm close enough.

"Enjoying my garden for as long as I can."

With it getting colder, all the flowers will start dying soon.

I drop a kiss on her cheek and take the place beside her. It reminds me a bit of Griff's place out here. Overflowing flower beds and small trees, a distinct fragrance on the air that I only ever associate with her.

"It's like you knew I was coming," I say.

"My Mom-senses were tingling."

"Please don't say tingling again."

"Fine." I can feel her steady gaze on me. "But I'm *sensing* something is going on with you."

"I've been here all of a minute—how do you do that?"

"I've known you every day of your life. It'd be more concerning if I couldn't read you."

Maybe. I mean, Griff and I can read each other easily. I guess when you love someone and pay enough attention, you can learn everything about them.

"You're right."

"I always am. Are you going to share with me?"

Always cuts right to the chase, I swear. I'm smiling before I can stop myself. "You know how you're always going on about me finding someone to spend my life with?"

"Yes ..."

"Well, I have."

"Oh, Heath …" She grasps my hand. "I'm so happy for you."

"Thanks. I'm just …"

She tilts her head. "You're not happy?"

I shake my head because that's definitely not it. "No, I am. It's complicated."

"How?"

"It's Griff."

When Mom doesn't say anything, I chance a look her way. She's watching her garden again, clearly running through an overload of thoughts. "I can't say that doesn't make sense."

"How so?"

"Well, you two have always loved each other." She laughs. "Is that what all that *Griff is my platonic life partner* bullshit was about?"

"Hey, that wasn't bullshit. At the time."

"Uh-huh."

"I'm serious." I nudge her. "Always gotta bust my balls."

"If I can't say tingling, you can't say balls."

"What would you prefer?" I ask innocently. "Nuts? Scrotum? Big, hairy testicles?"

She swears under her breath. "Why are you visiting again?"

"Do I need a reason? I always visit you."

"I know … though it's been less lately. I'm guessing Griff is the reason."

"He is." That guilt knocks me around again. "He shouldn't be though. I'm sorry."

She waves me away. "It's not your job to look after me."

"Dad asked me to make sure I did."

She smiles sadly. "Because he has a big heart. And he meant well, but he also wouldn't have wanted you to do it at the expense of your own happiness."

"I'm not."

"Heath ... you're the best son I could have ever asked for."

Her words settle something inside me. "You're a pretty okay mom yourself."

She tries to pin me with a look, but she's smiling. "You know I don't expect you to visit every weekend, don't you? I love seeing you, but I never want you to feel like you have to be here."

"I don't. I *want* to be." If only she wasn't so far away. "You know, I applied for a job up here. Training hotel staff. I did that because I wanted to be close to you."

"Before or after Griff happened?"

"Before." There's no way I can lie to her. "But now, I don't think I could take it even if they do ever call me back. So weekend drives are my only option."

"I know you worry."

"You're my mom. Of course I do."

She drums her fingers on her lips as she thinks. "Maybe Griff could come with you sometimes."

"I think he'd like that."

"And maybe ... maybe I need to start considering that this won't be my home forever."

"What do you ..."

"I'm getting old."

"You're not even seventy," I point out.

"And this house is too big for one person."

"You're going to move closer?"

She doesn't answer right away. "I don't know. I can't see me finding anywhere that feels like this place does."

I know what she means. Even though we moved a few times when I was younger and Mom and Dad only settled here after I moved out, it feels like home.

She can't give it up for anything less than perfection.

Thinking about my childhood reminds me of all the friends Mom still has in Kilborough though. "Can you please keep everything about me and Griff to yourself?"

"Of course, but why?"

"No one knows."

"Is there a reason for that?"

"Felix."

Understanding crosses her face, and she nods. "Griffin is worried about his reaction?"

"Of course. You know Fe."

Mom laughs. "I remember smuggling him donuts during his attempt at a hunger strike in the school cafeteria."

"He was the worst in middle school."

"How do you think I felt teaching him home ec? I've never met another student who could single-handedly burn everything."

Felix is one of a kind.

"Do you remember what that hunger strike was for?" I ask, straining my memory.

"Something about sausages. Who can remember now? He was going on about a new thing every week, it was impossible to keep up."

"And that's why Griff's worried. Felix is the best, but he's not exactly rational."

Mom shrugs. "Well, you're doing him a disservice by keeping it from him."

"What do you mean?"

"You're not giving him a chance to react and process. Maybe he'll be dramatic about it, but he also might surprise you. He's in college now; he has his chance to grow up."

I get what she's saying. "You're forgetting one thing. It's not my choice. That decision is all up to Griff, and I'm not going to push him either way."

She purses her lips, and I know she doesn't agree.

"Besides, Felix doesn't even know his parents aren't together."

"*What*?" Mom snaps, and I know she's not happy.

"Save it," I say before she can start ranting. "Griff hates it too, and maybe it's not what either of us would have done, but Griff and Poppy made the decision with Felix's best interests in mind. You can't ask for more from a parent."

"It's dishonest."

"So is Santa Claus."

"That's not the same thing, and you know it."

I wrap my arm around her shoulders and pull her in for a

side hug. "I know you care about me and want me to have the world, but I'm seriously okay with all of this. Griff needs time, and I'm happy to give it to him because I love him. The only thing getting me down is knowing I can't be there to help him through it."

"How did I create such an amazing human?"

"Are you kidding, lady? I practically raised myself."

She shoves me away, and I pinch her cheek, jerking away again when she tries to slap my hand. "You think you're *so* funny ..."

"Okay, so *maybe* I take after Dad in that way."

When she looks at me, her smile is warm. "In many more ways than that. Griff is very lucky to have you."

"And I'm lucky to have him. We just need to give him time."

"If it's what you think is best, then fine. But if he strings you along when I see him again—"

"I'll be sure to warn him about the fragile, old lady coming his way."

"Please ..." She sniffs. "I'm not even seventy yet."

"Nuh-uh. You can't throw my words back at me."

"Can and did. And if you think this fragile, old lady doesn't have ways to exact revenge, you better think again, kid."

"Sure thing. I'm very scared."

"You would be if I still had my Renaissance fair costumes," she grumbles.

"Those weapons weren't real."

She looks me up and down. "That's what you think."

All the weapons and costumes she used to keep locked up flash through my mind. "Please tell me you didn't have a real crossbow."

"Why would I do that?" she asks. "You know how I hate lying."

I hum, casting my eyes over the garden. It'll all be gone soon with the harsh weather coming in, and it gives me an idea. "Any chance you have some spare pots lying around?"

"In the shed, why?"

"Want to help me pot up some orchids? I want to take them to Griff."

The way she smiles makes me wish I'd fallen in love sooner.

DMC Group Chat

Griff: *Ever been so happy you're just waiting for the other shoe to drop?*

Art: *No. My life is all-around genuinely awesome.*

Payne: *Yes. After what my fucker ex did, I was wary about starting something new.*

Orson: *Beau was safe though. If there was ever a man who you could trust completely it's him.*

Griff: *Will not make an inappropriate comment about Beau.*

Orson: *Hey look, Griff held back!*

Payne: *He did. That's ... suspicious.*

Griff: *I'm growing up. Maturing. Griff 2.0.*

Art: *Awwww Daddy is so proud.*

Payne: *Gross.*

Orson: *No. Please no.*

Griff: *And I think the other shoe just dropped ...*

Chapter Thirty

GRIFF

My yawn stretches wide before I glance over at Heath with a dopey smile. He doesn't see me —he's too busy watching the sun rise as he sips from his coffee—but this moment is perfection. The calm before our day starts, quiet company with the person I love more than anyone other than my son. And maybe I haven't said that exact word to Heath yet, but he knows. He'd have to. Like how I know he feels exactly the same without him needing to say it either.

I can read it off his face every time he looks at me.

"Should probably start getting ready," he murmurs, the hand resting on my thigh squeezing tighter for a brief second.

"No," I whine. "Because then you have to get dressed and leave."

Heath chuckles. "You'll see me in two hours when I get to work."

"You clearly have no idea how long two hours is." I let my stare dip down over his bare chest.

Heath chuckles. "Okay, now I'm definitely leaving because I know that look, and if I don't go now, we'll end up naked and covered in cum."

"You say that like it's a bad thing."

He drops a kiss to the top of my head as he passes to go back inside. "You might own the place, but I still have a start time."

"We could use orgasms as time owed?" I suggest. "For every one you give me, you get to start an hour later."

"Wow, do you have tickets on yourself. You seriously think you could last out an hour?"

"I could probably come close."

"Pun intended?"

I flip him off, and after he gets changed, I watch Heath leave, trying not to be too down about it. I have no reason to be. Everything with us is exactly how I ever envisioned a future relationship going.

Except for one thing.

The secrecy.

Keeping him locked up in my place and not being able to touch him or kiss him when I want is a struggle. I meant what I said about not wanting him to be dragged into gossip, but at least if Poppy and Felix knew, I wouldn't have to be so careful all the time.

I'm just trying to figure out how many more weeks it is

until Felix is home when there are footsteps on the path ahead.

It's way too soon for Heath to be back, and I don't think he left anything so ...

Poppy appears between the trees with a worried look on her face.

That doesn't scream good news.

"Thank god you're up," she says as she crosses the courtyard.

"What's wrong?"

"Felix."

Oh, shit. "What happened? Is he okay?"

"I can never tell with him. I woke up to a voicemail saying that he was getting on a plane to fly home, but he didn't say why."

I blink at her. "He put himself on a plane?"

"It seems so. He used the emergency credit card we gave him."

What could possibly constitute as an emergency that he had to fly home immediately? It's Felix, so it could be *anything*, but the sinking in my gut doesn't feel great. "You don't think he found out. About us?"

"Fucking hell, I hope not. We'd never hear the end of it."

"So what do we do?"

"Maybe ..." She glances around. "Maybe we pretend we're still living together. At least until we know why he's running home."

For the first time since we decided to split, I don't want to cover up the truth. "No."

"What do you mean *no*?"

"I can't lie to him anymore."

Then Poppy does something she's done a hundred times before, but I never saw it for what it is. She looks at me like I'm stupid. "You're the one who wanted to wait. Who didn't think he could handle it."

"I know that," I say, keeping my tone level. "And we waited. We gave Felix everything he needed. His whole childhood was *his*. But he's an adult now, and he needs to understand that we're people too. I've put my life on hold this past year—"

"And I haven't?"

"We *both* have. And we can't do it anymore. It's not fair on any of us."

She looks me over. "Okay. Fine. But when he's upset—and he *will* be upset—I don't want you blaming this on me."

"Of course not."

Poppy takes a long breath. "Right. Well ... I guess it's the most official it's ever been."

"You okay with that?" I check. Not that it would make a difference.

"I am. I've ... I went on a date last weekend."

"Really?" I'm smiling before I realize it. "How did it go?"

"Awkward." She frowns. "Really awkward. But he wasn't sleazy, so I guess I got lucky there."

"I'm happy for you."

"Thanks. What about you? Looking to date, or still having the fun you never got to when we were younger?"

Now would be the perfect moment to tell her about Heath, but I can't do it without clearing it with him first. "I think ... I'm working on something."

"Mysterious ... okay." She checks her watch. "His flight lands soon. You going to come with me?"

"I better. I don't want you to have to lie about where I am."

"Thanks."

I nod, then duck inside to get changed and send Heath a quick text that Felix is on his way and I won't be in until later. I'm beyond excited to see my son again, to grab him in a hug and never let him go, but I'm dreading his sudden return home.

If word has gotten back to him that we've split, who the fuck knows how he's going to handle that we didn't tell him? Jumping on the first flight home doesn't fill me with confidence, and when I do the quick math, his flight would have had to have left around one in the morning.

What is that boy thinking?

And do I really want to know?

Felix's plane is late. It's exactly what my fraying nerves need.

But the second he walks through departures, broad grin on his face, the reasons for him being here don't matter. Two months is the longest I've gone without seeing him, and he clearly feels the same because there's no hesitation when I hold out my arms and he steps into them. I squeeze the stuffing out of him.

"I've missed you, kid," I say before dropping a kiss on his curls.

"Okay, old man." He rolls his eyes, then steps aside and hugs Poppy as well.

I scoop his weekend bag from the floor and lead the way out to the car.

Felix is behaving like he always does. There's no awkwardness, no tension waiting to unleash. Poppy and I share a look as we climb into the car, waiting for him to spill on his sudden return home, but as soon as the car starts, he launches into a play-by-play of his first taste of college life.

The whole way back to Kilborough, I wish I was driving so I could make out his expression in the rearview mirror. There's nothing in his tone to give me any hints about his visit, and the few times I manage a glimpse back at him, he's as happy and excitable as ever.

This is ... strange. If he didn't rush back here for something, that means he randomly decided to put himself on a plane in the middle of the night.

There has to be something up.

But instead of letting us know what it is, he's regurgitating some joke his math professor told them, and given the fact it's not even remotely funny, it can only mean one thing. Felix is avoiding.

My gut sinks. If he's avoiding, it means he's either hurt

or embarrassed. Angry Felix doesn't have an issue with exploding.

I doubt this has anything to with the divorce, and the odds of telling him about it while he's already upset aren't good.

Dammit. I try to hold off my uneasiness as I watch the trees on the side of the road fly past. I promised myself. I told Poppy we'd spill, no matter what, but faced with my kid and knowing I'm going to upset him makes the whole thing so much harder.

That's the whole reason why you're still in this mess.

The voice trying to reason with my doubt sounds a hell of a lot like Heath. Not surprising considering my choice not to tell Felix probably impacts him the most. I can't expect Heath to keep hiding, and if I'm honest with myself … the distance between me and Fe since he left hasn't been all physical.

Instead of going home, where it'll be very obvious I've moved out based on the bare rooms, Poppy drives us to Killer Brew. The lunch rush has already started, but we still manage to get a booth inside, and as I slide into one side, with Poppy and Felix opposite me, I consider ordering a beer to get through this.

I know I haven't done anything wrong, but with this table between us, it feels like it's me versus them.

Thankfully, Poppy starts talking first.

"What's going on, Fe?"

He clears his throat, looking around the room like he's seeing it after years rather than months. "Nothing. I just missed my parents ..." The high pitch to his tone gives his lie away.

"Bullshit," I say. "I'm sure you did, but that's not why you're here."

The excitement from being home seems to melt away as a wariness takes over.

My gut twists at the look he pins me with, and before he can say a damn thing, I'm already about to apologize. But he doesn't call us out on the divorce.

"I have something I need to tell you." He drops my stare, focusing on the table instead.

"You couldn't have done it over the phone?" Poppy asks.

And the way Felix shakes his head clues me in on what this might be about. He gasps air to steady his breathing as he avoids eye contact.

"Go ahead," I prompt him. My voice already sounds scratchy with emotion, but if this is what I think it is ... the fact he's so nervous means I've failed him.

When Poppy and I discussed whether or not to tell Felix I'm bi, we ultimately decided it wasn't worth confusing him. We were married, and that wasn't changing.

But ... I swallow, resisting the urge to take his hand as he shreds his coaster to pieces.

"This ... this is something I kinda need to do face-to-face." He blows out a breath, followed by a shaky laugh. "I don't even know why I'm so nervous when you won't care, but—"

His rambling makes me give in to my urge, and I reach over and cover his hand with mine. "You're okay. Tell us."

His piercing blue eyes meet mine. "I'm gay."

And with those two words, I have the unexpected urge to cry. I have no idea where it comes from or why. It's this overwhelming build of emotion, and I'm not even sure it's completely tied to Felix's announcement or just, well, everything.

"Oh, honey …" Poppy wraps an arm around his shoulders. "We don't care who you're attracted to. Not when—" Her eyes shoot to mine, and I know she's asking for permission.

I nod, my hand tightening over Felix's.

"Your father is bisexual."

Felix's gaze shoots back to me.

"I'm sorry we didn't tell you," I say. "You might not have had to go through all this yourself."

"Wow." And like that, my son is shocked into silence, which isn't something that happens often.

"Are you okay?" I ask.

"Yes." Felix hurries to pat his eyes, and his curls catch the overhead light, making them look redder than usual. "But, like, bi … what does that mean for you two?"

I always assumed that if I ever told Felix, that would be one of the questions I'd need to answer, but I'd always pictured the answer being "nothing different."

Except, everything is different now.

And even though we've never specifically lied to him about our relationship ending, not letting him know what was going on is just as bad. I can feel Poppy watching me, waiting for my go-ahead that this is really when I want everything to come out, but I know that if I let this moment pass, I'm going to keep finding excuses to put off the difficult conversation, and short-term peace for me isn't worth Poppy and Heath having to put their lives on hold.

I take a steadying breath. "In general, it means nothing. I've been happily married to your mother for twenty years. She's made me happy."

His eyes narrow. "*Made?*"

"We also have news," I tell him. "Though it's completely unconnected to my sexuality."

Felix stiffens, pulling away from us both, and I know he's already figured it out too.

"We've decided it's time to separate."

And while I always knew it'd be hard, saying those words and watching his whole face crumple with confusion almost rips out my heart. "Mom?"

Poppy smiles. "It's okay. We've been talking about this for a while now and—"

"*A while?*"

"Inside voice," she reminds him, not rising to his level. "And yes, it's been a while. Now, are you going to throw a tantrum, or will you let us explain?"

I shrink at her frank words. I've never been able to handle him like that, but sometimes the situation calls for it, and apparently, this is one of those times. I watch him wrestle with all the emotion trying to explode outward, and in the end, he settles for a glare and a curt nod.

"We haven't been completely happy, and during your senior year, we established that the marriage wasn't working.

We've been taking small steps, and when you left for college, your father moved out"—Felix turns his glare on me—"so we could trial being apart and make sure it was what we wanted."

"And?" he snaps.

"It's what's best for the both of us."

"This ... I just—I ..." His foot is tapping madly under the table.

"We understand this is a shock," I tell him. "But we still care about each other, and more importantly, we still care about you."

"I don't get it. If I didn't go to college, would you still be together?"

"No," Poppy says, leaving no room to argue. "We held off on any big steps until you got through high school, but this was always coming."

He scoffs.

"Fe ..." I try to take his hand again, but he snatches it away. This isn't going the way I'd hoped it would. The last thing I ever wanted was for this to hurt him, but I know we couldn't have pretended forever.

"Out of curiosity, what part are you upset about?" Poppy asks.

"Are you *kidding*? You're getting *divorced*."

"Ah," she says. "So you wanted us to be miserable so that you weren't inconvenienced. I get it."

"No, that's ..."

"That's what?" She's calling him on his shit in a way I never could.

"Not right. You're trying to turn this back on me. You were happy together. I lived with you—I saw it."

"You also saw the fighting," I point out.

He looks like he wants to retaliate but isn't sure how.

"It's okay. We tried to hide it, but I know you knew."

"You haven't fought for ages though." Finally, the shock is being replaced by uncertainty.

"About a year." I nod. "The same time we decided that we weren't working anymore."

He squirms in his seat, looking like he has to pee, and it reminds me so much of when he was younger and would refuse to stop having fun until he almost wouldn't make it to the bathroom in time. He's an adult now, but he'll always be my kid.

And right now, he has no idea of anything.

"Hey," I say to get his attention. "I know this is hard to hear, but we're both happy. We're both on good terms. We'll all still do holidays together and hang out together. The only major change is that we live apart now."

"What if you start seeing other people?" he throws back. "How am I supposed to process that?" His big eyes pin me with a pleading look that makes me want to take everything back.

"Your friends have never broken up with their partners and found someone else?" Poppy asks.

"That's different. They're not my *parents*. It feels like … it's like …"

"You need time to process this," Poppy tells him, and

this time, he lets her pull him into another side hug. "That's all."

He cringes but doesn't argue, thank fuck, because I'm still working through the pain in his voice when he talked about other people. I want to tell them about Heath. To get it all out there. But I haven't checked in yet, and it feels like throwing a lit match onto gasoline.

Felix is calming down now, but I can't not say *anything*.

So instead, I figure it's best to get him used to the idea as soon as possible.

I clear my throat. "We have started seeing other people." The words are hard to say. "Both of us. And we've both talked about it and about seeing each other with someone else, and we're okay. But we need you to be as well, because there's a good chance we'll find someone we're serious about, and when that happens, we both need you to accept it."

He's glaring again, and it's eating me up inside.

"*Please*, Fe. You're the most important person in our lives. Always. There's no way we'll be able to move on unless we have your support in this."

"You're asking me to be okay with seeing my parents with someone else."

"Yes." No point skirting around the issue. "Or at least to be open to the idea."

"Fine," he says, even though he doesn't look happy about it. "Date whoever, but I don't want to meet them."

"Felix ..."

He shrugs, then crosses his arms. "Those are my terms."

Well, that's not exactly how we wanted it to go. I glance at Poppy, who gives me the type of exasperated look she gets with the both of us. I guess this is the best we can hope for.

"Until it's serious," I add on. "You won't meet anyone unless things are serious." Because there's no way I'm hiding Heath for any longer than I need to.

He thinks it over for a minute before giving a jerky nod.

I almost melt with relief.

And now that the separation is out there, I can breathe again.

"Sorry for stealing news day," I say because that part didn't go well. "Just so you know, we both love you and support whoever you're attracted to."

"Hmm, yeah." He screws up his face. "I can't believe my dad is bi. Have you—" He cuts off, going red. "Never mind."

I chuckle, knowing exactly where he was going with that question. "That's not information you need about your parents."

"You're right."

Poppy suddenly spins in her seat so she's facing Felix straight on. "Hang on. Why the big need to tell us right away? You got on a plane partway through the night, without calling, without knowing if we could pick you up—"

"I needed to get it off my chest, okay?" His words are fast, slightly high-pitched, and his face is burning the brightest red yet.

"Let me guess, you were at a party last night?" I ask.

"Yes ..."

I half laugh, half groan as I drag my hand over my face. Kilborough isn't a backward town. It's very queer-friendly, but the number of queer people here is small, and so far as I know, none of the other boys in Felix's year were out. It's very possible he's only figuring it out because ... well, I remember my first time having sex. I'd wanted to shout it from the fucking rooftops it felt so good. That feeling plus alcohol equals exactly the type of rash decisions that would have him jump on a plane in the middle of the night.

"What does the party have to do with anything?" Poppy asks.

"Let's just say the reason Felix got on that plane isn't information parents need to know about their kids."

Understanding fills Poppy's face right as Felix dramatically face-plants onto the table.

I pat his head. "Well, this has been a successful lunch conversation."

They both flip me off.

Chapter Thirty-One

HEATH

"Uncle Heath!"

I look up from where I'm handwriting our guest welcome cards and find Felix at the reception door, arms extended above his head.

A mixture of happiness and guilt hits me all at once. I love Felix—he's like a nephew to me in all the ways that count. I've never had to discipline or deal with the meltdowns; I've been there for the fun. I've loved seeing him grow up.

And now he's a gangly eighteen-year-old, I understand where Griff was coming from when he mentioned feeling old.

Felix crosses reception and pulls me into a quick hug. "I can't believe you didn't tell me," he says, trying and failing to sound offended.

My head shoots toward Griff because I thought he wasn't telling people about us yet, let alone Felix. And Felix ... he doesn't sound pissed.

Relief overtakes the warring feelings a whole second before Griff says, "C'mon, Fe. You know Heath would never betray my trust like that."

His ... trust?

Realization dawns on me. "The divorce."

"Yeah," Felix answers even though I hadn't asked a question. "What did you think I was talking about?"

"Just ... that. Tell me what's going on with you. Why are you rewarding us with your presence?"

The confused look he's giving me is replaced by uncertainty. "I ..." He glances at his dad and back at me again. "I did what you suggested."

"You did?" Right before Felix left for college, he told me he was questioning his sexuality, and I mentioned how college was where I figured it all out.

"Wait." Griff steps forward to join us. "Suggested? What do you mean?"

"I went to Uncle Heath for advice. You know, since he's gay and I thought I was too."

"And what was the advice?"

The low, suspicious tone and the way Griff narrows his eyes at me causes the kind of bodily reactions I do not want to be having around Felix. I move back behind the desk and drop into the chair. "All I said was that if he's unsure, college is a good place to experiment."

Felix is practically vibrating out of his skin. "Yep, and

you were right. I have answers. And I maybe got a little excited about it and jumped on a plane to fly home and tell Mom and Dad."

My heart fucking swells. "I'm so happy for you. Welcome to the club."

His cheeks are red as he meets my hand in a high five.

"Now, tell the truth. You're avoiding the guy, aren't you?"

He tries to squash back a smile as he glares at me exactly like Griff was doing earlier. "I have no idea what you mean. Felix Andrews doesn't avoid people."

"Right." I narrow my eyes.

He shifts.

I shake my head in disbelief that he's lying to me.

"Fine!" He dramatically throws his hands up. "There were some, umm, complications, let's say. Nothing to worry about, no problems, everything is *fine* and *functional* and—"

Oooh. I know exactly where he's going with this. "Let me guess, you shot off like a rocket launcher in only a couple of seconds?"

"I don't need to hear this," Griff splutters.

Felix drapes himself over the desk with a long, drawn-out groan. "I can never look him in the eyes again after that."

"The good thing about college is you probably won't have to."

One of his eyes pops open, and it's the one feature he got from Griff. They're startlingly blue. "Keep saying things like that."

"It's perfectly normal. It happens to us all."

"I know you're lying, but I appreciate it. Can we go out for breakfast now? Ooh, or brunch. Now I'm gay, I can do that, right? What about Dad though? He's only half-gay, so does that mean he only gets to half brunch? Maybe we should leave him behind."

Griff swipes at Felix's head. "I'm zero parts gay, thanks. And I'll do brunch if I wanna."

"I guess we better go, then." He turns to head for the door when Griff catches his collar.

"Nice try, but you're not getting out of this. You want to book an emergency flight home, you can work to pay it off. We'll do lunch. I'm sure you gays won't waste away before then."

"That's what you think," Felix mutters, looking completely put out.

I'm smiling so hard my cheeks hurt, but it comes with a tinge of sadness as well. This is what I stand to lose if Felix isn't happy about me and Griff being together. He loves us both, I know that, but it doesn't mean he'll love the idea of us getting it on.

What a fucking mess.

They leave to get Felix set up with one of the cleaners, and half an hour later, when I'm locked away in the office, Griff walks in and closes the door behind him.

He doesn't say a thing as he crosses the room and pulls me into a long kiss. I relax into it, almost taken aback by how the neediness inside me settles. He feels right. He feels like home. It isn't something I've ever experienced before, which is why we're taking the risk. Being together feels like the most right thing I've ever done with my life.

"I'm sorry," he says against my lips.

I pull back. "For what?"

"Ditching you yesterday. Springing Felix on you today. It's a lot, but—"

"Griff." I laugh softly. "Are you seriously apologizing for putting your family first?"

"Ah ..." He thinks for a moment. "I guess I am."

My sweet man. "Don't. That's not something you ever have to worry about, because I know you. I know how important they are to you, like I know how important I am to you. It's not a competition."

He lets out a long exhale and drops his forehead to my shoulder. "Thank you. I tried to keep you filled in, but yesterday got so busy, and there was so much going on."

"I get it." I run my hand through his hair, knowing he needs the comfort. "I appreciated every message."

"I wanted to tell them about us so bad."

"You already had the divorce and Felix coming out. And, uh, apparently you coming out to him too. That's more than enough to process. It's not a rush."

"I just want everything out there."

"No," I remind him. "You want everything out there in the *right way*. And it will happen. I'm not going anywhere. Are you?"

He's shaking his head as he pulls back to look at me. "Never if I have anything to say about it."

"See, we have time." I press a kiss to his forehead, his

nose, and then his lips. "And in the meantime, we have this. Now, stop stressing."

"I can't help it," he says, a teasing glint in his eyes. "I didn't get laid last night. I'm all tense."

"If you can get away tonight, I'll make it worth your effort."

"Oh, really ... how?"

"Hmm ..." I pretend to think about it, then lean in and whisper my suggestion into his ear.

Griff stiffens. "Yep. I'm in. Can honestly say I've never even thought to try that before. Maybe we should call it a half day—"

I pull away quickly. "Don't even think about it. You need to go and pick up that produce from Blakely farms so the kitchen will be stocked over the weekend, and then I have a list of repairs for you to work on."

Griff pretends to sob.

"That's what you get for taking a day off."

"Fine," he grumbles as he stands and swipes the keys to the Magnolia Ridge truck. "I'll be back for lunch."

"Can't wait."

I'm not being sarcastic either. I imagine Felix's trip home will be a fast one—his specialty, apparently—so spending that time with them is invaluable to me. If Griff and me being together ruined their relationship, I'd never forgive myself, but I have to believe that Felix will want us both to be happy. Sure, past experience might not support that belief, but people grow up quickly during their college years.

Griff gets back right on time, and we end up at a small restaurant down from Killer Brew. It's on the boardwalk, and the tables outside have a nice breeze blowing in. Now that Felix is settled, he's been giving me a full rundown on college life, talking so fast I don't think he's stopped for a breath. I share a fond smile with Griff because I really do love this kid. He's loud and talkative and completely him. Half his curls are pulled up in a knot at the top of his head, and I can tell he's had his full dark eyebrows waxed since he left. He's somehow nothing like Griff and Poppy while still managing to be everything like them.

"So tell us about this guy," I cut in.

"Well, school happens to be not that far from where the big ol' navy ships dock, and my friend and I happened to be walking past when all the sailors came in—"

"Nope." Griff holds up a hand. "I don't need to know anything else."

"I didn't take you for a prude, Griff," I say.

"I am when it's my son we're talking about."

"You should be happy he's open about this stuff," I point out. "Sex positivity is a healthy thing."

"And he can be positive about it … when I'm not around."

"Naww … is Griff realizing his son is all grown up?" I ask, putting on a baby voice.

"Griff is wanting out of this conversation." He tries to turn his attention back to the menu.

"I'll have to keep those delicate sensitivities in mind."

"Why? So you can use them to taunt me some more?"

I pump my eyebrows. "Always need more ammunition in the arsenal."

"Such a dick."

"And yet, you love me."

"I've definitely changed my mind on that."

"What ..." I start at Felix's voice and turn back to him, sensing Griff do the same. Felix has the same little crease that Griff gets dimpling his forehead as he looks from his dad to me and back again. "What's happening here?"

"We're getting lunch," I say as casually as I can.

Griff doesn't answer, and it's like I can *feel* him sweating from here.

I nudge the menu toward both of them. "What are we all having?"

"The same as always," Felix says, brushing his menu aside. "But ... you guys are ... being weird."

His words are coming out stilted, like he's choosing each one carefully.

"It's your dad," I say. "He's always weird."

Especially like *right now* when we could use a little less weirdness. Griff still hasn't said anything, and now *I'm* starting to sweat. Felix's attention has narrowed in on his father, and when I finally let myself peek over at Griff, I find he's imitating a fish.

I pray to the gods of unpleasant bar stains that Griff isn't about to do what I think he is.

"What's going on, Dad?"

"Maybe he's stroking out," I suggest before helpfully

waving my hand in front of Griff's face. "Hello, Earth to Griffin—"

Felix bats my hand away. "And you think *he's* being weird." Understanding floods Felix's face, and he jerks right back in his seat. "Holy shit. How long?"

"What?"

He turns back to Griff. "How long have you and Uncle Heath—" A shudder races through him. "No. Nope. Just ... *urk.*"

Griff finds his voice about a hundred hours too late. "Felix ..."

"Just answer the fucking question. And if you try to lie, how pissed I was over the divorce won't even come close to this."

Griff exhales. "Shortly after you left."

Something that looks like betrayal crosses Felix's face, and I'm totally unprepared for how hard it hits me.

"Does Mom know?"

"No. I didn't want to say anything unless we were sure about this."

"And are you?" he fires back. "Because I would have thought you'd be sure before you basically committed incest."

"It isn't even close to that," I say.

"He's my dad. You're my uncle. What else would you call it?"

"Still two people who are totally unrelated."

"Maybe to you two. But now I have to be all these are my two dads, oh, but he's also my uncle. Long story."

"Or you just leave the uncle part out," I snap. I don't mean to, but *fuck*, Griff is back to being silent. I'd been hoping so hard that Felix could be happy for us. That maybe the few months he's been away would have helped him to grow up. But shit. What happens if Felix totally flies off the handle? Is that going to be something Griff could get over? Could *I*?

"I don't want to have this conversation with *you*," Felix says, and I swear his tone breaks my heart.

For some reason, that jolts Griff out of it.

"Then have it with me. But listen up carefully because I'm only saying this once. I love you. I want you to be happy, but like I said yesterday, it's time for me to live my life. I know you don't want to hear this, but as much as your mother and I love each other, we weren't right together. Our marriage was commitment and responsibility. I'll never regret the time we had together, but I need to move on from that. So you can either get on board, or every time we see each other will be filled with tension. I don't want that. The two of you are the most important people in my life, and without you both, I don't know who I'd be."

Felix is scowling, and I know he doesn't want to hear any of this. I know he's prone to reacting and thinking later, and I know this is all a lot for him to process.

"You don't have to be happy with this," I say. "Maybe you completely hate me. Maybe you'll never want to see my face again. But can't you try, Fe? Your dad put his life on hold for an entire year for you. Can't you at least try and accept us for him?"

"I didn't force him to do that."

"No one said you did."

He lifts his hand to his mouth and bites his thumbnail. "Mom's going to be hurt."

"It's possible," Griff says. "But she's smart, and you know she can be frustratingly levelheaded about things. I'm hoping this is one of them."

"What if she hates you?" Felix asks. "Am I going to have to take sides?"

"Never. But how your mom reacts has nothing to do with us," Griff says. "Only you get to decide if this is going to affect your relationship with me because no matter what, I'm not turning my back on you. Your mom never would either."

"This is ... I can't ..."

"Is it easier if you pretend that we're still friends?" I ask. "Because we won't be affectionate around you if it makes you uncomfortable."

"Affection—" Felix cringes. "No. Nope. This is too weird for me. I'm out."

"Felix ..." But before I can stand, he's gone from the table and disappears out of the restaurant and onto the street.

"Fuck," Griff mutters but doesn't move.

"Aren't you going to go after him?"

Griff hesitates. "He needs to let off some steam first."

"Yeah, and you do know how he's going to do that, right?"

"How?"

"I can guarantee you he's going straight to Poppy."

Griff pales. "You think?"

My heart aches for how blissfully naive he is at times. "Felix is hurting. What does he do when he's hurting?"

"He lashes out."

"Exactly."

"Shit. I better go." He gives me a quick kiss before he jumps up and leaves, and it's not until he disappears from sight that I realize what he just did.

He kissed me.

In a public place.

And judging by the eyes I can feel on me, people definitely noticed.

Chapter Thirty-Two

GRIFF

Of course I can't catch a break, and by the time I get outside, Felix has disappeared. Goddamn it. Surely he wouldn't be running straight to Poppy—that's a conversation I need to have with her, because I can only imagine how irritated I'd be to find out she was dating someone and everyone knew before me.

A part of me is kicking myself for not saying something sooner, but Heath and I were right that we needed the time to ourselves. Getting the freedom to work out what we wanted and how things would go without outside interference has been good for us.

Now I need to convince Poppy and Felix of that.

I take the car we came in, shooting out a silent apology to Heath for leaving him stranded, and make the drive to my old house. The whole way there, I keep hoping to spot Felix, but either the kid grew wings, or he ordered a car to pick him up.

When I arrive, Poppy's car is out the front, letting me know she's home, and I let out a grunt of frustration at having to do this in a rush before I unbuckle my seat belt and jump out of the car.

My gut is a twisted mess, and I can't stop raking my hand through my hair as I wait for Poppy to let me in. After what seems like the longest time, I hear her footsteps approaching, and then the door opens.

"Griff?" The surprise in her tone gives me hope that Felix hasn't gotten to her yet ... and then her expression falls. "Got something to tell me?"

Fuck.

"Can I come in?"

She steps aside. "It's your house too."

I pass her and walk down the hall to the living room, the whole while feeling like I'm in an out-of-body experience. This was my home for almost twenty years, and yet after only a few months away, it's a completely foreign house. I have no emotional attachment to it anymore.

"Would you like a drink?" she asks.

I wave her off and drop into an armchair. "I have a feeling I won't be here long."

She gives a weird hum and sits down opposite me.

"I take it Felix told you, then?"

"Felix?" She cocks her head. "I thought he was out with you."

"No, he left. He didn't come here?"

She sighs. "Did he see it too?"

And ... now I'm lost. "See what too?"

"The kiss, Griff. What were you thinking?"

"Kiss ..." What's she talking about?

"Why do I feel like we're talking about two different things here?" she asks.

"I ..." I tilt my head. "You haven't spoken to Felix?"

"No. But now I'm worried about why he left."

Well, thank fuck he's not here yet. "He sort of figured something out and wasn't happy about it."

"You and Heath?"

I blink at her in surprise. "You know?"

"Well, what did you think would happen when you kissed him in the middle of a crowded restaurant? Lucy saw you and called me straightaway."

Oh ... That hadn't even registered with me; I'd been working on autopilot. "I'm so, so sorry."

"You should be."

"This isn't how I wanted you to find out."

"Through town gossip? It wasn't my favorite way either, if I'm honest. But that's not what you should be sorry about."

"Then what—"

She throws up her hands. "How could you do it to him?"

"Felix?"

"*Heath*. Jesus, keep up. No one knows we've separated, and then people see you kissing him—they're going to assume the worst. He doesn't deserve that."

It takes me a moment for her words to sink in. "You ... you don't care?"

She makes a few attempts at words and keeps cutting herself off. "Of course I *care*. It's going to be strange for a while. Heath is practically family. But I love you both, and I want you to be happy, so do I care that you're moving on with *him*? Truthfully, Griff, I don't think there's anyone you're better suited for."

All the fight seeps from my body as I'm hit with relief. "Shit, Poppy, I—"

"Did you think I was going to be hurt?"

"I wasn't sure which way it would go. You don't usually have big emotional reactions to things, but I figured if you thought there was something going on behind your back ..."

"I know there wasn't."

"How can you be so sure?" I bring myself to meet her eyes, and it occurs to me that this is the part I need her to be certain of.

"Because I know you both. Neither of you are capable of hurting people like that, and also ... you are the worst liar I've ever met."

I laugh through my loud exhale. "Thanks for understanding."

"I'm offended you thought I wouldn't."

We share a smile. "Can I hug you?"

"If you must."

We both stand and meet in the middle of the room. And as I'm squeezing the shit out of her, she murmurs, "You know, you were an excellent choice for my first husband."

"And you were an excellent choice for my first wife."

She snorts and pulls back. "*Only* wife. I will be very shocked if you and Heath aren't forever."

"Dad?"

We both glance toward Felix's voice. He's watching us from the doorway, anxiously shifting from one foot to the other.

"What are you doing here?" he asks.

"What I should have done sooner."

His gaze flicks toward Poppy and back to me again. "Did you tell her?"

"I did."

"And ...?" His question hovers between us as he glances back at Poppy.

"And what?" she counters.

"You're not pissed that he kept it from you?"

"What right would I have to be pissed about that?" As always, Poppy is unnervingly calm. I respect the hell out of her for it, and I'm so glad that Heath understands and appreciates that she'll always be part of my life.

"He's your *husband*."

"Ex-husband. And I lost all right to say anything about his relationships when we decided to end things. I knew I'd have to come to terms with seeing him happy with someone else, and I am."

Felix scowls.

"But I've also had the last year to get used to the idea, and this is all still new for you."

And like that, Felix's annoyance melts away, and he looks at me like he did when he was younger and had hurt himself.

"Fe ..." I open my arms, and after a moment of hesitation, he steps forward into them.

"I don't want things to change," he whispers.

"I struggle with it too. But I promise, this is the good kind. And now, all three of us get to support each other through some big life changes."

He pulls back with a confused look.

"You support your mother and me through dating and our new relationships, and we support you through basically the same."

"Oh no," he groans, but there's a tinge of melodrama about the way he says it that gives me hope. "If you're with Unc—*Heath*, and then I get a boyfriend too, does that mean I'm copying you? And if I'm copying you are you—*eww*—cool? I think I need to sit down."

I shove him gently. "I've always been cool, you little shit."

"Really, Dad? You couldn't have waited to get your gay on until I did it first? You're ruining my big queer coming out."

"Good to know college hasn't changed you."

"Next time I'm with a guy, I'll have the mental imagery of my dad and uncle hooking up." He gags and lets his tongue loll out.

"You mean I don't have to even be there to keep you celibate? This gets better and better."

Felix turns to Poppy, bottom lip sticking out. "I think I'm ready to go back to school now."

"I hope you've learned your lesson about spontaneous flights home," she says.

"I can promise you, hand on heart, that I will never, ever do that again."

Chapter Thirty-Three

HEATH

After taking an Uber back to work, I lock myself in the office for the rest of the day. I have no idea how Griff is going with Felix and Poppy, but stressing about it isn't going to help either of us. So instead of regretting that I didn't go with him for support, I pour all of my focus into chipping away at my ever-growing to-do list.

We need to find someone to replace my old role, but I swear since we had that conversation, everything keeps escalating and becoming more time sensitive.

We had a win with that busted pipe, but the couple we moved weren't overly thrilled at all the changes, so left us neutral feedback. I wanted to flip them off and tell them never to come back after how hard we worked to accommodate everyone, but the number one rule of customer service is that you can't make everyone happy.

Not even when you bend over backward for those assholes.

I prop my elbows on the desk before burying my face into my hands. We're running this place into the ground. I can see it coming, but no matter how hard I work, I can't turn the ship.

Poor Griff loves this place.

Like everyone keeps pointing out, I'll do anything for him.

Including not letting this place go downhill.

I set aside my to-do list and write out what our biggest problems are so far, along with what their fixes could be. Then I list them in order of priority.

First thing is first: replacing my old job, which I'm pretty sure Michelle could do in her sleep, so then we'd need to replace Michelle ...

I spend the afternoon typing up a job listing as well as an updated role description for Michelle. I'm so deep in concentration that when my phone rings, I almost jump for my dear life.

I give my heart a second to settle before I answer.

"Hello, is that Heath Turner?"

"It is."

"Heath, this is Marcos from Premier Hotel. You interviewed with us a few months ago."

Holy shit. My gut flips when I consider what this call could be. "I remember."

"Sorry we've taken so long to get back to you. Our hotel has recently been through some restructuring, and the role you interviewed for no longer exists."

Of course it doesn't. Which is probably a good thing because it means not being trapped between Mom and Griff. "No problem. I understand."

"We actually have a newly created position that we think you'd be perfect for. It's our executive guest relations manager, and essentially, you'd run the team responsible for accommodating our most valued guests." The man goes on for a while about the team and the hotel, and there isn't a good point for me to jump in and tell him that I'm not interested in a new position. I'm manager here now, and Griff needs me. It's as simple as that.

I try to block out the guilt at putting Griff before Mom. I know she'd never hold it against me; I know she wants me to be happy, but that doesn't make it any easier to choose not to be there for her, especially since I promised Dad I would be.

I tune back in as the guy mentions the salary and swear my eyes almost fall out at the number. "I'm sorry, *what*?"

He chuckles and repeats himself.

That's ... that's almost double what I'm earning here.

Fuck. Double fuck.

"You still with me?" he asks.

"Yeah, I'm here."

"I know this is sudden," he says, but I can pick up the smug tone of someone who thinks they've won you over. And to be fair, if Griff and I hadn't decided to give this a go,

I would have said yes by now. "I'm happy for you to take time to think about it, and I'll send you through all of the details in writing. Off the record, we haven't taken this public yet because you were the one we wanted for the role, but we can only give you until Monday for an answer. Then I'll need to start advertising."

"Yeah ... I mean, of course."

He rattles off a few details, then confirms my email address and gets me to check I have his number to call if I have questions.

And I do have questions.

Many, many questions.

He's not the one who has answers for me though.

Do I want this job? The honest answer is yes.

Yes, *because* it's closer to Mom.

Yes, *because* it's a lot more money.

Yes, *because* there will be a whole team of people I'll be working with rather than everything falling on me.

But it doesn't matter how many of those yes, *because* answers there are. There's one giant no as well.

As in, no, *because* if I take it, I'll lose Griff.

More than that, I'll lose this place. I love the people, I love working here, and I love every day that I get up and arrive at Magnolia Ridge, it's like coming home. I won't get that anywhere else.

The current relationship I have with Griff is only new, but *we* aren't. The two of us have made it through so much together, and no matter what happens with the resort, we'll make it through that together too.

I open the email as soon as it's sent to me and read the whole thing from start to finish. It's a fantastic opportunity, and if they'd offered me this right after my interview, I would have said yes. Without question.

That makes me think the delay was for a reason because while I can tell it's great, and I should be excited ... I'm not. Things are stressful and borderline overwhelming here, but the thought of walking away feels *wrong*.

Relief sweeps through me.

Stressful or not, this is where I want to be.

And when a text comes through from Griff to tell me Poppy knows and everything is okay, I immediately shut the computer down.

He's waiting for me at his place, and even though he's only a few hundred yards away, I can't get there fast enough.

Chapter Thirty-Four

GRIFF

The second Heath walks through my door, I grab him in a bear hug and crush him against me.

"I take it everything went well." His voice is muffled against my shoulder, and instead of answering, I squeeze tighter. My hands follow the planes of his back as I breathe in his sweet cologne.

All the anxiety and worry from the last few months is completely gone. No lying. No secrets. Just ... so much fucking relief.

Heath pulls back, and I belatedly notice the pot he's holding. "For you."

"Orchids? Damn, I can never manage to get those to grow around here." I've tried. *So* many times.

He gives me a soft kiss as he passes to place the orchids in the center of my table, and I get this moment of *wow*, this is my life now. How did I get so lucky?

"Holy shit," I say.

"What?"

"I just realized that I have nothing to stress about anymore." The feeling goes to my head. I can't stop smiling.

Heath doesn't look like he shares my relief. "What about the business?"

"Don't worry about that." I wave the worry away. "It'll take time, but we'll sort it out."

"I'm glad you're so confident."

"I am, and ... I have something for you too."

Surprise lights up his face. "Oh yeah, what's that?"

I'm excited as I open the cupboard in the kitchen I've hidden his present in and pull it out. "I finished it."

The flower is light wood, and I've painted gold streaks around each petal. It's rough in some places, but I'm so happy with how it turned out after so long without practice.

Besides, rough or not, I made it with Heath in mind. Because I knew he'd love it, and the way his face lights up confirms it.

"This is amazing."

"It's okay," I say awkwardly, my cheeks feeling hot. "I need more practice, but you said you didn't care how it turned out, so ..."

"And I meant it, but I love it. For real." He squeezes it in his hands. "I'm happy to see you happy again."

"I am, because I have you. We're gonna be the dream team, baby."

"We already were, man. Us fucking doesn't change that."

"But it's more than fucking. Right?" Even though we've talked about this, I want to make sure that now it's real and out there, he isn't having second thoughts.

"Well, half the town probably knows by now, so it's a little late to walk away."

I cup his face. "You could though. If you wanted to. I'd never force you to stay."

"You force me to stay every day."

"What?"

He laughs and grabs my ass. "By being so sexy."

I puff up at the praise. "Glad to know my old ass still has it."

"Your old ass is the best thing about you."

"My old cock resents that."

His smile spreads over his face. "Luckily, that's the part I'm interested in tonight."

I remember what he whispered in my ear earlier, before everything went down, and the idea has my dick thickening. "You really think we can do it?"

"Not sure, I've never tried before. But I have been doing my research."

"Research?"

"I've watched a *lot* of porn, okay? And from what I've seen, you're well equipped for the task."

Given I've never been with another man, it's safe to say I've never tried docking before. I have no idea how this is supposed to work, or even if it'd feel good, but thank fuck Heath knows what he's doing. The best I can hope for is that it's not awkward or uncomfortable, and I know Heath would stop if it's not working, but I also *want* it to feel good because I like that this is a first we get to experience together.

I push his jacket from his shoulders. "Guess there's nothing stopping us from trying, then, is there?"

Heath's mouth finds mine, and we kiss, slow and deep, as he backs me toward the bedroom. I work the buttons of his shirt open, and he follows by stripping me out of mine. We take our time, hands and mouths exploring each other's bodies before I drop to my knees and mouth at his V while I work open his pants and push them down his legs.

His presence and the scent of his skin is so familiar it warms my insides. I wrap my arms around his waist before resting my cheek against his stomach and letting myself take in the moment. It's so fucking perfectly intimate I wish we could stay like this forever.

Heath's fingers card through my hair, and I lean into the touch. "I love you, Griff."

I look up at his husky tone, heart doing somersaults. This isn't the first time we've said that. Maybe not even since we started sleeping together, but this time feels different. Both heavier and lighter at the same time. "I love you so fucking much too."

I shove to my feet and haul him into a kiss that's so deep I feel like I'm eating his face. Heath claws at my sweats, roughly shoving them and my briefs down, while I work his underwear down his body as well.

His naked body tangles against mine as we fall against

the bed. I can't get close enough to him, can't touch and kiss and hold him enough to settle this burning need in my gut.

I love him.

"You have no idea how much I want you."

His words are laughable because the way he feels about me couldn't come close to how I feel about him. Heath is ... everything. He's long summers together. He's support and kindness. Hard work and a smart mouth. A man I've always admired. He's second chances and hope. He's my future.

Heath reaches between us and strokes my cock. "It's apparently better if you're not all the way hard," he says.

"I don't think that's possible around you."

His grin is fast, melting away into lust when he glances down and gives my foreskin an experimental tug. It feels ... different. A slight stretch, pleasant tingles ... mostly my cock likes the attention.

"I wanna suck you," he says.

"That's not helping with operation half chub."

He laughs. "Okay. Right. Sorry. I'll hold off mentioning how sexy your cock is then."

"Now you're setting me up to fail."

But despite my words, I let my eyes fall closed and try to focus on anything other than the small tugs and his long, careful strokes.

"You ready?" he asks.

"I think so."

"Maybe you should do it. So I don't hurt you."

Probably a good idea. I climb on top and take over while Heath grips the base of his cock and holds it steady. There's some primal need inside me that loves seeing our cocks lined up like that. That gets off on the very obvious arousal we feel for each other. I pull back my foreskin and take a moment to rub the heads of our cocks together, watching as a dot of precum appears at Heath's tip before I smear it between us.

"Fucking tease."

"I think I could get off like this," I say. "Just rubbing my cock over yours."

"We can frot later. I want you wrapped around me."

With a long groan, I press my cock tighter against his, then roll my foreskin up. I'm not expecting much, but somehow, I get it over his tip and partway down his cock. And it feels ... I don't even know how to describe it.

Close, intense, intimate. The sight is a thousand times hotter than how it feels, which is helping with not getting all the way hard.

Then I glimpse Heath's face. His eyebrows are knotted, mouth hanging open with his stare trained on our cocks. He takes my hand and shifts it so I'm wrapped partially around me and partially around him.

"Feel good?" I ask.

"It's like ..." He huffs a breath while he tries to find the words. "Suction. So hot."

I tighten my grip and stroke us, rewarded with a heavy gasp from him.

"Yes, just like that."

There's nothing but appreciative noises between us as we both watch my hand. The more I watch, the more I stretch myself over him and press us tighter together, the hotter it gets. And hearing the proof of how good it feels for him is driving me crazy. As much as I want to watch, I want to be close to him more.

I lean in and catch his mouth with mine. Whereas sex is usually fast and hot, this is slower, different, but every bit as sexy. We take our time to work ourselves together, to kiss long and deep, to indulge in each other's bodies. Heath's hands roam over my back to my ass, fingers dipping into my crack and brushing against my hole.

Every nerve in my body feels alight. His tongue takes control, his fingertips brush every sensitive place on my body, even as his breathing gets shallower, faster, and his whispered gasps between kisses take on a husky note.

He breaks from my mouth. "This is insane. Like I'm so desperate to come, but I'm hovering right next to it. Like you're edging me."

I squeeze us, and he moans, the sound sending pleasure right to my balls.

Our eyes lock, noses touching, mouths one hot breath away from each other. I jack us slowly, sensually, trying not to get too hard and end this all now. "Tell me more."

"Fuck, Griff ..." he breathes, giving a pump of his hips. "It's so hot. I feel like I'm fucking your cock."

I groan.

"I'm getting so close."

"Literally all of my effort is being put into *not* getting too close and ruining it."

His laugh is weighed down by lust, and he reaches between us. "Let me ... I saw ..."

He takes over, and I plant my arms on either side of him as Heath strokes us, and then he gives a little twist.

"*Ah* ..."

"Good?"

"Yes. Do it again."

His strokes are firm and slow, alternating with that little twist that sends ripples through my cock. My aim to not get too hard is going way out the window, and within seconds of this magic trick, he has me close.

He gives the sheathed heads of our cocks a firm squeeze. "Oh, you really like that. I can feel it."

"I'm not the only one." The stickiness rubbing together isn't all from me.

"Fuck no, you're not." He kisses me quickly. "I wanna see again."

I eagerly push up onto my hands so I can see as well. This is probably the hottest part. Feeling his tip rubbing against mine, the shivery pleasure as my skin passes over his, and the sight of us joined, connected as one, it's as hot visually as sexually, and my cock is hardening to a point it'll be a struggle to keep going.

"You need to come. Please."

"So close ..." His hips give these tiny thrusts in time with his hand, and it's so hot to watch him working us like that, I can't keep still either. It really does look like he's fucking my cock, and the visual sends shivers through my limbs.

"Griff ..." he moans, and then his dick jerks as he comes.

Feeling each spurt against my sensitive head is too much. My balls tighten, my thighs tense, and when Heath jacks me off hard and fast, I'm barely fucking his fist for a few seconds before my orgasm crashes into me. I cover him in my release, holding myself up long enough to watch my cum paint his skin, and then I collapse against his body.

He lets out a long exhale, dropping his head back on my pillow. "That was wild."

"Definitely one of your best ideas yet."

"Stick around. There's plenty more where that came from."

I give myself a second to catch my breath before I shift to meet his eyes. "I want to," I say. "Stick around. I can't imagine life without you. I'm in this for the long haul."

"Thank fuck for that, otherwise you would have had a stalker situation on your hands."

I laugh and kiss him again. Because I can. Because I can't get enough.

He's perfect.

"Never leave me," I say.

"Never going to." Heath reaches up to tug my ear, and I practically maul him as I kiss him again.

Chapter Thirty-Five

HEATH

I don't know what to do. It's been two days since I received that job offer I should have said no to, but it's still sitting on my computer. The problem is, I can't have Griff and the job. It's not possible. And I'll cut my arm off before I walk away from him.

But turning them down makes me feel ... sad.

I miss Mom. She's all I have left, and I want her to know how much I love her, and while I know Dad would never want me to keep my promise to him above my own happiness, I wish it didn't have to be one or the other. Choosing between Griff and my only remaining parent shouldn't be a position I'm in.

But there isn't a single part of me that wants to take this job.

I let out a long breath and open the email to read for the

fortieth time all the ways I'm fucking up in life. More money, less responsibility, closer to Mom ... but no Griff. And I'm one hundred percent okay with saying I'm giving all of this up in order to have him.

The door to the office opens, and Griff sticks his head inside. "Ready for lunch?"

Work-wise, yes, but ...

"Actually, there's something I want your help with."

His blue eyes widen, but he steps inside and closes the door without question. When he rounds the desk to take the seat beside me, I nod at the screen.

"What's this ..." He starts to read, and the longer he reads, the more his mouth drops. "You're leaving?"

"What? No. No, definitely not." Fuck, I should have thought that through.

"But it says you interviewed and ... you're not happy here?"

"That's the thing. I am. So happy, and I swear this isn't about that."

He blinks at me, looking so damn vulnerable I can't help but pull him closer to give him a reassuring kiss.

"Stop looking at me like that."

"Like what?"

"Like I just cut your nut sac off."

Finally, a small twitch of his lips. "I think that would hurt less than losing you."

"Aww, Griffy. Are you saying I'm more important to you than your balls?"

"On my love scale, you're one step higher than my genitals. Congratulations."

"Now that's true romance."

He snorts with amusement, but that worry line creeps back in.

"I'm not going anywhere," I hurry to reassure him. "I don't want to. I love it here, and now we're together, nothing could get me to walk away. But right before the split, before I knew Poppy was leaving the resort and we'd end up together, I ... well, after Dad died, I wanted to be closer to Mom. I've been driving up to visit and keep her company a lot, but it's a long drive to do multiple times a week."

"I didn't know you were going so often."

"Because I didn't tell you."

He looks back at the screen. "They're offering you a lot."

I close out of the job. "It doesn't matter what they're offering me. Yeah, I wasn't sure I wanted to do guest relations forever, but I'm a manager now, and I have you."

"Then why are you telling me this?"

"Because I haven't said no yet."

His mouth drops again.

"I'm *going* to. But every time I'm about to write the words, I remember Mom is up there all by herself, and I feel like a shit son that I'm putting my happiness before hers."

"Has she said she'd want you to do anything else?"

"Well, no—"

"Because she wouldn't." Griff takes my hand. "I know

your mom, and I know she wouldn't want you to do something that makes you unhappy."

He's right. Mom's said it a thousand times, but it doesn't make shaking these feelings any easier. "She's getting older. I don't want something to happen and to regret all the times I didn't go see her."

"I know."

"It'd be so much easier if she'd move back here."

"It would be."

I lean closer to Griff, and he wraps an arm around me.

"I'm not pressuring you," he says. "Because I wouldn't want you to do something that makes you unhappy either. But if you need me here while you turn them down, for support or whatever, I can be."

That actually sounds like a perfect plan. "Okay." I reopen my emails.

"You don't have to do it now," he hurries to say.

"Yes, I do. Because it's not fair for me to keep them waiting. I'm not taking the job, and at least with you here, you can smother me in love when I feel like the worst son in history."

He hesitates a second. "Deal."

I type out my response and hold my breath as I hit Send. "Okay, done."

Griff drags me out of my chair and wraps me up in his big arms. "Smothered yet?"

"Bit tighter." I sigh as he crushes me against him. "I wish I didn't have to choose."

"I know. But we'll figure it out. Promise."

Chapter Thirty-Six

GRIFF

The uneasy feeling weighing on me doesn't leave all day. I had no idea Heath felt that way, and as his partner, it's my job to know. It's my job to support him through whatever he needs.

I failed.

And while I might have helped him with turning the job down, I'm also not convinced it's what he really wanted. I'm taking him at his word because it's not up to me to make choices for him, but if I can do something about the things bugging him, I fucking will.

His mom is problem number one, but his job comes a close second.

At least with his job, that's something within my power to fix.

My idea might not be what he had in mind, but I might

as well clear it with Poppy before I ask if he's interested. If he is, I think we'll solve a lot of problems at once.

Poppy and I drop Felix at the airport, and it's easier to say goodbye this time, knowing he'll be back to visit in a couple of weeks. Now that all the secrets I was keeping are out there, my only worries are about giving Heath everything he needs.

"I've had an idea," I tell Poppy as we climb back in her car to head home. "And feel free to say no to this, but it seems like where things are headed anyway."

"I'm listening."

The words are hard to get out because I'm putting so much hope into this plan that if she says no, I'm back to square one. "You want out of Magnolia Ridge, correct?"

"I do …"

"Well, as it stands, working there or not, you're still tied to it."

"I know."

"So, what if you weren't anymore?"

It takes her a second. "You want to buy me out."

"Not me. I don't want that kind of pressure, but …"

"Heath."

Of course she'd know. She's too damn smart for her own good sometimes. "Now, before you say I'm thinking with my dick or whatever—"

"I wasn't going to say that." She checks her mirror as she indicates to switch lanes. "Heath loves the resort, and we both know he's far more qualified to run it than you are."

"By a long shot."

"Okay, then, I'll set up a meeting with him."

I'd expected Poppy to eventually say yes, but I thought it might take some convincing to get her there. "Not that I don't love how this conversation is going, but I didn't think it would be that easy."

She laughs. "Did you want me to complain? Push back?"

"I'm not sure what I expected, actually."

"Logically, selling to him rather than someone else makes the most sense. He knows the business, he knows what he's getting into, and he's not some random hookup of yours. There won't be any discounts; it's all happening aboveboard, and I'll be paid what it's worth."

I wouldn't have thought about suggesting otherwise. "You don't think mixing business with a new relationship is a bad idea?"

"It might be. Who knows? But once I'm bought out, that's going to be your problem, and if you're happy to do this, I'm not going to stop it. Besides, Heath is more or less family. I've always thought so."

"Kinda sounds gross when you say that."

"Familyyy," she drags out.

"You're going to have fun with that, aren't you?"

"Damn right."

"Well, remember that whatever shit you give me, Heath and I will give back double when you start dating."

"I'd expect nothing less."

When I get back home, it's already dark, but my front door is wide open, light spilling out into the courtyard.

I lean against the doorframe, smile splitting my face when I find Heath cooking in nothing more than an apron.

"Geez, I'd go away more often if this is what I get to come home to." I take a second to look around, appreciating for the first time all the things he's slowly snuck into my house. Potted plants fill the corners and countertops, there are paintings on the walls, and I even have a fucking rug in the area designated as my living space. It's still minimalist, but it's warm. Homey.

"Whatever do you mean?" he teases before turning his back on me to plate something up. I can't stop myself from crossing the space and crowding up behind him. My hands immediately drop to his round ass and squeeze.

"Excuse me, sir, this is an entirely inappropriate way to handle one of your employees."

I snigger and trail kisses along his neck, loving the way he pushes back into me, wanting more. "Careful." I grab his hips. "Press your ass against my cock one more time and I'll be forced to bend you over this counter and have my way with you."

He groans. "As much as I love the idea, we need to table that before dinner goes cold."

"Fuck dinner. I'd rather fuck you."

Heath laughs and eases me away from him, then hands me a bowl. "Carry this, would you?"

Resigned to no sex for the moment, I help him load up the table with everything for tacos and salad. Sitting there, at the table I made, on chairs I made, eating dinner Heath made, is paradise.

I almost don't want to interrupt it with conversation, but hopefully, he'll take my idea as good news and not a pity offer.

"I was talking to Poppy today," I say.

He smiles. "I should hope so. It would have been a boring-as-fuck car ride if you were silent."

I want to bite back at the sarcasm, but I force myself to stay on topic. "She wants to sell her share of the resort."

"What?"

"To you."

Heath watches me carefully for a moment. "This was your idea, wasn't it?"

"I started the conversation, but she's the one who said there was no one better for it."

He sets his taco on his plate and leans back. It's one of those rare times I can't read his face, but this is a decision he needs to make on his own.

"There's no pressure from me either way," I tell him. "The sale was always going to happen one day, but Poppy was in no rush to just offload to whoever. If you're interested, she's happy to sell now. If you're not, she'll hold on to it until the right person comes along."

"And you don't want to buy her out?" he asks.

"Fuck no. It would mean another mortgage, and I have no interest in that at all."

Heath takes a long moment, not saying anything, so I reach for the hand he has resting on the table. "You don't need to answer now. Have a think about it. But to be clear, this has nothing to do with our relationship and everything to do with you earning it."

A small smile works its way onto his face. "We'd finally be equals."

I quickly shake my head. "Impossible. Buying her out or not, when it comes to work, I'll never be on your level."

"Everyone has different skills, and I think it's a good thing that we're complete opposites. We balance each other out."

"Like two halves of one whole." My lips twitch because I never thought I'd be corny enough to believe in two people *completing* each other, but fuck if Heath and I don't come close.

He nods. "I'm going to do it."

"Yeah?"

Heath lifts my hand and presses a kiss to my knuckles. "Yeah, I ..." He lets out a long breath. "Wow. You're basically giving me everything I've ever wanted."

Except for one thing. "If I could make your mom move back, I'd do that too."

"I know, and ..." He glances around the room. "Now I feel terrible even saying this, but I did plan dinner to talk to you about something as well. And you've already done so much."

"You've held me together for years. Whatever it is, the answer is yes."

"Hold on there, cowboy. It's a big ask," he says.

"I don't care."

"Even if it means moving in with me?"

I blink at him, lost for words. It doesn't even occur to me to ask if it's too soon. With us, it's more like it's way, way too late. "My answer stands."

"In that case ... how would you feel about my mom moving in here?"

"You think she would?"

"She wants somewhere small and homey, with a huge garden. This fits. Plus, it's right where I work, so I'll be able to make sure she has everything she needs."

I tilt my head. "That's not the reason you asked me to move in, is it? Because she can have this place. I'll find somewhere—"

He's out of his chair and in my lap before I can process him moving. Heath's arms wrap around me, and his mouth finds mine in a searing kiss that lasts so long my head goes fuzzy. Finally, he pulls back. "Nope. You're not taking it back now. You said you'd move in, and I'm holding you to it."

My heart swells. "I couldn't think of anything more perfect."

"I dunno ..." He rolls his hips, ass pressing teasingly against my groin. "Your idea of bending me over the counter sounded perfect to me."

I laugh. "What happened to dinner first?"

His hot breath ghosts over my ear. "It's definitely time for dessert."

Epilogue

HEATH

ONE YEAR LATER

"Holy shit, Uncle Heath, you got Dad into a suit." Felix pretends to inspect the inside of Griff's jacket.

"What are you doing?" Griff asks.

"Looking for flannel. It has to be in here somewhere."

Griff shoves him away while I turn back to the mirror to anxiously check my tie. We're in Art's office that's been converted into a temporary change room for me and Griff. "Leave your dad alone. And would you cool it with the *uncle* shit?"

"What would you prefer I called you?" Felix bats his eyelashes my way. "*Daddy*?"

"Don't start," Griff warns him.

"Call me that and you'll put me in an early grave." I shudder. Since coming out, Felix hasn't held back in embracing his full self. He's a loudmouthed, snarky twink, who tells us way more than we need to know about his sex life. It's only gotten worse since he moved out of the dorm and into a share house with four other guys. There was a rough patch when he first went back to school, after finding out the news, where his grades slipped and he was ... not himself. But thank fuck that was over with quickly.

"It's okay," Felix says. "I had way too much fun telling everyone I was coming home to be best man at my dad and uncle's wedding."

I don't doubt for a second that's exactly what he told people.

There's a soft knock on the door, giving us an out to *that* conversation. I'm expecting Mom, who thankfully moved into the cottage, so I get to see her every day, but Orson pokes his head inside.

"You both look great," he says. "Just wanted to let you know the flowers are set up and everything is ready to go. Art said he'll let the guests up when you're ready."

"Thanks so much," I say, but Orson has Felix's attention.

"Is mechanic daddy here?"

"Stay away from him." Griff points at Felix, but it's a

mistake. Warning Felix not to do something only encourages him.

Orson's normally happy face pulls tight. "Ford is ... somewhere."

I grab Felix before he can disappear. "Wedding first, flirting later."

"Fine." He sighs. "Not even my dad yet and you're already a buzzkill."

"Keep that up, young man, and there'll be no drinking tonight either."

"It's disgusting how perfect you two are for each other." Felix moves to the door. "I'll let Art know you're ready."

Felix ducks out, and I have no doubt he's gone to find Ford to flirt with, but since it means a quiet moment with Griff, I'm not about to point that out.

I move closer to my husband-to-be.

"You feeling okay?"

He smiles down at me, blue eyes bright, natural grays in place, and I can read him as well as I ever could.

I'm ready.

I stroke his cheek, but when he leans up to kiss me, I quickly turn my head. "Nope. We're not kissing until you get a ring on my finger. Geez, how cheap do you think I am?"

"Well, the other day, you sucked my dick for half of the ice cream I was eating, so I'm noticing holes in your argument."

"Yeah, but you like my holes."

"Some of the best things about you."

"I'm listening if you want to tell me all the other good things about me."

"There'll be time for that later," he points out.

Yeah, like the rest of our lives. The thought sends flutters through me.

I never saw myself as someone who would get settled down, and after his divorce, I wasn't sure if Griff would ever want that either. But I asked on a whim one night, and he said yes, and so far, it's the best decision I ever made.

My joke about Griff having to leave their divorced club fell flat when Art informed me it's DMC for life, in a borderline threatening tone. I'm sure he was joking. He had to be. But I will definitely be keeping an eye on him.

I'm still not convinced Art hasn't spiked the drinks with his love juices.

Griff's eyes are soft as he watches me, and the same butterflies that kick in every time I'm around him flood my gut.

He reaches up to tug my ear.

I love you, his expression says.

"I love you too."

THANKS FOR READING PLATONIC RULEBOOK!

The next book in the Divorced Men's Club series is coming in November. Check it out here:
Budding Attraction

And if you want to read about Griff's son, Felix, grab his book here:
The Dating Disaster

To keep up to date with future releases, come join Saxon's Sweethearts.

www.facebook.com/groups/saxonssweethearts/

My Freebies

Do you love friends to lovers?
Second chances or fake relationships?
I have three bonus freebies available!

**Making Him Mine
(A Divorced Men's Club prequel)
Friends with Benefits
(A Never Just Friends novella)
Total Fabrication**

These short stories are only available to my reader list so
follow the link below and join the gang!

https://www.subscribepage.com/saxonjames

Other Books By Saxon James

DIVORCED MEN'S CLUB SERIES:

Roommate Arrangement

Platonic Rulebook

Budding Attraction

FRAT WARS SERIES:

Frat Wars: King of Thieves

Frat Wars: Master of Mayhem

Frat Wars: Presidential Chaos

NEVER JUST FRIENDS SERIES:

Just Friends

Fake Friends

Getting Friendly

Friendly Fire

Bonus Short: Friends with Benefits

LOVE'S A GAMBLE SERIES:

Good Times & Tan Lines

Bet on Me

Calling Your Bluff

CU HOCKEY SERIES WITH EDEN FINLEY:

Power Plays & Straight A's

Face Offs & Cheap Shots

Goal Lines & First Times

Line Mates & Study Dates

Puck Drills & Quick Thrills

PUCKBOYS SERIES WITH EDEN FINLEY:

Egotistical Puckboy

Irresponsible Puckboy

And if you're after something a little sweeter, don't forget my YA pen name

S. M. James.

These books are chock full of adorable, flawed characters with big hearts.

https://geni.us/smjames

Want More From Me?

Follow Saxon James on any of the platforms below.
www.saxonjamesauthor.com
www.facebook.com/thesaxonjames/
www.amazon.com/Saxon-James/e/B082TP7BR7
www.bookbub.com/profile/saxon-james
www.instagram.com/saxonjameswrites/

Acknowledgments

As with any book, this one took a hell of a lot of people to make happen.

First, my cover designer Story Styling Cover Designs did a fantastic job on making this smoking hot cover.

To Sandra at One Love Editing for my amazing edits.

Lori Parks, you were a gem as always with my proof read and I always appreciate how timely you are with your work.

Thanks to my wonderful PA, Charity VanHuss for wrangling my scattered self on a daily basis.

Eden Finley, your notes and ongoing commentary were fucking incredible, and thank you for letting me pick your brain while talking absolute smack at each other. You're the bestest bestie I could ever ask for.

To all of my amazing betas, you helped make this book so much stronger. Your support is incredible and I really appreciate it!

And of course, thanks to my fam bam. To my husband who constantly frees up time for me to write, and to my kids whose neediness reminds me the real word exists.

Printed in the USA
CPSIA information can be obtained
at www.ICGtesting.com
LVHW040215061023
760346LV00007B/12/J